GOOD MOON RISING

THE SIREN ISLAND SERIES, BOOK FOUR

TRICIA O'MALLEY

LOVEWRITE PUBLISHING

GOOD MOON RISING
The Siren Island Series
Book Four

"We all come from the sea, but we are not all of the sea…"
– Frosty Hesson

CHAPTER 1

"*W*hat's with you today?"

"What do you mean?" Jolie caught the other side of the fitted sheet Mirra tossed to her, and together they made up the bed for the new arrival to the Laughing Mermaid. It was their slow season, as summers tended to be just short of unbearable with the heat, and they were pleased to have a long-term booking for one of their rooms.

"Your aura is off. Did you not sleep well?"

"My aura is fine, Mirra. Like you can even see auras. I think you're making it up." Jolie was constantly miffed that her and Mirra's magicks had manifested differently.

Like being mermaid wasn't magick enough?

It rankled when Mirra would flit around and diagnose people's ailments or personalities based on their aura colors. And most annoying of all was the fact that Mirra was more often right than wrong.

"You always say that. Jealous much? I don't say anything about your healing powers."

"That's because you're a healer too."

"Not as good as you are, Jolie, and you know it. Now, tell me what's bothering you." Mirra's beautiful face creased in concern as she studied her sister. Though they were born twins, they were anything but identical except for the fact that they were both breathtakingly beautiful. Mirra, light to Jolie's dark, was blond, ethereal, and soft of heart. Jolie, with her riot of dark curls, sharp blue eyes, and salacious wit, could cut through most men with a look and make them drop to their knees and beg. Mirra preferred a gentler approach; her men were often found composing poetry and planning romantic picnics. Jolie preferred the more rough-and-tumble types, and was just as happy wrapping her legs around a man in leathers on a motorcycle as she was sneaking into the captain's quarters on a ship. As sisters, they were yin to each other's yang, and a deep love abided between the two. When Mirra expressed concern, Jolie did her best to listen.

"I don't know…" Jolie shrugged, smoothing a duvet, brilliant green shot through with white threads, on the foot of the bed. "I'm just off today."

"Did you have bad dreams again?"

"Well, not the same one. A different one this time, actually."

"Tell me," Mirra said, moving to the sideboard to unload the basket of supplies they used to stock the rooms. Fresh fruit for the basket on the table, waters for the mini-fridge, tea and coffee by the kettle. They moved automatically, having done this change-over many times, and it soothed Jolie to work while she talked.

"This dream was about Irmine. About the night she lost him."

"Ah. That's an old one."

"It is."

"Why do you think it's come back now?"

"For me it feels like the dream focuses on the anguish of her loss and then her determination to make something of her life. It doesn't just end on the night she lost him, but skips ahead to how she's used that love to grow other areas of her life."

"So… a lesson then? How pain can lead to good?"

"Or maybe that we should still take a chance on love? Even if we can't know what the future will hold."

"I like that interpretation. It's more along the lines of how I like to think." Mirra, ever the optimist, beamed at Jolie.

"I know, which is why I'm surprised I'm thinking it."

"Will you look for love then?"

It was a constant discussion between the sisters. Their mother, Irma, had also lost their father tragically and had mourned him ever since. It had left the girls wary of deeper relationships – Jolie preferred to love 'em and leave 'em – but at the same time, their mother urged them to grab on and love as fiercely as they could.

Finding someone worthy of that love, however, was a whole different issue.

"Haven't I always?"

At that, Mirra let out a pretty peal of laughter, like the softest of bells chiming, and shook her head at Jolie.

"You most certainly have not. You've always looked for Mr. Right Now, and danced away from anything more serious. And plenty a man has wanted something more serious with you."

"I know." Jolie sighed, completely confident in her ability to ensnare men. "I haven't met the right man yet."

"How would you know? You barely give them a chance."

"O ye of the ol' aura readings... can't you tell? When you know, you know."

"I think you've grown bored and men come too easily to do your bidding. You need someone who'll stand up to you."

"I've dated plenty of bad boys," Jolie said, tying back the white linen curtains that framed the glass balcony doors. Beyond the doors, the sea called to her – like it always did, a primal pulse that beat deep in her soul – and Jolie took a moment to look out at the water.

"Bad boys that you could drop to their knees. You wrap every man around your finger. After a while, even that has to grow boring."

"I'll let you know when it does, darling."

"Shall we swim?" Mirra came to stand by her sister, and wrapped her arm around Jolie's waist. She knew the water soothed as much as it excited, and was always a surefire cure for whatever ailed them.

"Yes – the room's finished and everything else is touched up. I'll work out my angst in the water and then we can greet our delightful guest... what's his name again?"

"Dr. Theodore Macalister."

"Oh, a doctor? Sounds perfect for you, Mirra."

"You know the rules…" Mirra shot Jolie a look of censure over her shoulder.

"Right, right, don't sleep with the guests. Got it."

"Do you? Because Mom didn't make that rule because of me."

"Well, it was in place long before I shagged anyone here, so it's not because I broke it."

"No! You don't think –" Mirra gasped, turning on the staircase to laugh up at Jolie.

"Mirra! Of course! You can't think she's been celibate since our father died, can you?"

"I'd prefer not to think of it at all, really," Mirra said, a faint blush tinging her cheeks.

"Neither do I."

"Well, she may have grieved our father's death, but the woman is still living. And I'm sure she has her own needs, despite what you may think about those."

"You've got a good heart, Mirra. Much better than my cold and black one." Jolie laughed and bounced down the last couple of steps. "Let's go to the water. The call is particularly strong today."

"To the water then," Mirra agreed – but the concern didn't leave her voice.

CHAPTER 2

heodore Macalister hiked the strap of his serviceable duffle bag over one shoulder and the strap of his camping pack over the other. With a tan canvas-brimmed hat to shade himself, a sweat-wicking shirt, and breathable shorts, he was as comfortable as could be in the open-air airport of Siren Island. His eyes skimmed over the tourists who fanned themselves madly, having planned poorly for their arrival in a humid climate, and he shook his head slightly. Didn't people ever consider where their final destination would be? There was nothing worse than being unprepared, as far as he was concerned. He checked his trusty Swiss Army watch – no fancy Rolex for him, no matter how much his father tried to push him into purchasing a nicer watch – and saw that he was just a few minutes early for when Irma from the Laughing Mermaid was supposed to meet him.

When he'd stumbled upon the website for the lovely little inn, it had seemed serendipitous – but, charmed by the pictures and hooked by the name, he'd called to inquire about long-term rates. Irma had been very accommodating, due to their low-season, she'd said, and before he'd known it, he had set his summer plans to research the myths of the sirens of Siren Island. As a literature professor at Harvard University, he was particularly interested in mythology, and the sirens were at the top of his list to research. He'd earned the summer off, having taught for ten years – including summer programs – and rarely taking trips that weren't for work.

Not like *this* trip wasn't for work, too, but he'd built some time in for relaxation as well. He needed the vacation. His family worried for him; Theodore's mother chided him that he was working himself to the bone – and for what? He already had all the money he'd ever need. An early-round investment in a dotcom company that had been bought out had set him up for life. When a life free from the worry of making money had presented itself, Theodore had turned to working for love instead. And his first love? Well, it had always been books.

Sure, he'd been the nerdy kid kicking around the playground with a book in front of his nose. He couldn't even count the number of times he'd had his glasses broken, his book snatched from his hands, or been given a black eye or two. It was the way of things, he supposed. Some would say he was still dorky, but he no longer cared what anyone else thought – though if he was honest, he still had his own internal demons to deal with. Otherwise, Theodore lived life on his terms, doing what he loved, and he liked to think he'd helped a geeky kid or two find their way in life as well.

He pushed his glasses up with his finger and blinked as

the transition lenses tinted darker when he stepped into the sunshine.

"Theodore?" A woman – surely a supermodel if he'd ever seen one – straightened from where she leaned against a dusty pickup truck. Her long white hair hung in a loose braid over her shoulder, and her slender body was wrapped in a flowing pink dress. Bracelets jingled at her wrists when she waved to him, and if he didn't know better, he would have thought he'd found his first land-mermaid.

"That's me. Irma?"

"Yes. Welcome to Siren Island. May I help you with your bags?"

"No ma'am, I've got them. And may I say, you are just as lovely as a sunset over still waters."

"That's quite sweet of you, thank you. If I were twenty years younger, I'd thank you in a different way."

It took Theodore a beat to realize she was flirting with him, and his face flushed. It still flustered him when women paid attention to him, no matter how far he'd come from being the nerdy kid on the playground with no friends. At least he'd gotten better at hiding it.

"And I – or any man – would be a fool to pass that offer up."

"It's a right shame. But you're not for me, so I'll just admire you from afar and appreciate your good manners," Irma said, smiling at him. He had automatically rounded the truck to hold the driver's side door open for her.

"My mother was a stickler for manners."

"Sounds like she raised you right. Where are you from, Dr. Theodore Macalister?" Irma asked as she started the truck, her bracelets jingling as she shifted into gear and zipped from the parking lot at a startling speed.

"Call me Ted, please. And I'm from Vermont originally."

"Vermont? I hear it's lovely there."

"It is. We've got our own unique brand of people in Vermont, and I do love going back to visit my family." Ted kept his eyes trained on the sea, hoping to see something magickal spring from its waters. The sea always delivered surprises to him, and he never failed to be enchanted by her. Maybe it was because he'd grown up landlocked, or maybe it was the delight he found in ocean-based myths, but the sea felt like home to him.

"Where's home, if not Vermont?"

"Ah, not too far from there. I'm in Boston now."

"Big city guy?" Irma cast a surprised look at him as the truck bumped from a paved road to a dirt one.

"Not my favorite, no, but work takes me there. And I can find enough nature to be satisfied. I live on the Charles River, and as long as I'm close to water, I'm happy."

"Then you'll be ecstatic at the Laughing Mermaid."

"From the pictures online, I gather that I will. Thank you again for offering the long-term pricing. That was very nice of you."

"We're happy to do it. Less work for us to turn over rooms during low season. The villa is just up the way." Irma nodded to a white villa tucked among several breezy palms and skidded the truck to a stop in a cloud of dust. Ted got out as quickly as he could, but Irma had already slung his backpack over her shoulder.

"Please, let me," Ted protested, but Irma just laughed up at him.

"I'm stronger than I look. Let's get you settled so you can relax."

"Yes, ma'am."

Ted followed Irma up a beautiful wood staircase, then down a bright, airy hallway to an arched doorway.

"This is your room," Irma said, pushing it open and walking in to place his pack on the luggage stand. Ted followed and let out a low whistle. The room was done up in soothing whites and vibrant greens, leaving any other color to come from the shocking blue of the sea outside the balcony doors. A splashy rug in a vibrant green palm-leaf pattern and several potted plants tucked in corners added a tropical feel to the room; the bed frame was bamboo, and sheer white curtains framed the windows. It was perfect – not too fussy or distracting – and the low-slung chairs on the balcony begged for someone to kick their feet up and while away the hours looking out to the ocean.

"There's a welcome book with all the pertinent information here." Irma gestured to a desk with a small leather book. "Wifi code, phone numbers, and all that. Will you need a cell phone?"

"I have mine set for international."

"Perfect. Our numbers are in there. I suggest programming them in case you need us for anything while you're out."

"Thank you."

"We've added a welcome pack of food to your fridge, so you don't need to worry about running to get food first thing."

"I appreciate that. That helps a lot, because I still have to figure out my transportation situation. I was thinking I might hire a scooter."

"It's an option. Or we can work a deal with some friends and their truck if you'd like. We know someone who helps property-manage the homes of people who don't live on the island full-time. Some of them like to rent their cars out so they don't sit and rust for months at a time."

"That'd be perfect, thanks."

"Is there anything else you need right now?"

"I think I'm all set. I'll get settled in and maybe take a walk on the beach."

"Don't forget your sunscreen. It's hot out there," Irma said, walking to the door and pointing to a key hanging on a hook. "Key's here. We have our own suites downstairs, so if you need anything, please don't hesitate to ask. I hope you'll join us for a drink one of these nights?"

"I'd love to, thank you." Ted wanted to ask about the 'we' she kept referring to, but Irma was already gone, closing the door silently behind her. Exceptionally pleased with his choice, Ted busied himself unpacking and putting things in order. He liked to know where everything was, and in under an hour he had his clothes sorted; his workbooks, computers, and technology tucked away in the desk; and his swim trunks on. A flicker of movement caught his eye as he smeared reef-safe sunscreen on his arms, and Ted turned to walk to the balcony.

He promptly dropped the bottle of lotion at his feet.

A goddess if he'd ever seen one, a woman emerged from the water, her dark hair slicked back and so long it almost hit her waist. Her curvaceous body was clad in the tiniest scraps of red material he'd ever had the joy to look upon, which barely contained her considerable assets. His mouth went dry as he watched her saunter up the sand, turning to laugh back at someone behind her. When another woman emerged from the water, Ted swallowed as sweat broke out on his brow. He'd seen his fair share of beautiful women – hell, you couldn't walk ten paces in Boston without a stunner turning your head – but these women were something else.

His eyes were drawn back to the dark-haired woman. He watched her unabashedly, for he felt hidden in the shadows of the balcony. She was the stuff dreams were made of – no, fantasies, really – and his hands itched for a pencil to sketch this moment into his brain. No earthly woman could be this stunning, could she?

Heat flashed over his face when she turned and looked him dead in the eyes. Caught staring, Ted's face flushed with heat and he was glad for the hat that shaded his face – surely she couldn't see his blush from down there. Smiling up at him, the goddess blew him a cheeky kiss before continuing her saunter inside.

Ted dropped to the low-slung chair and took a few moments to just breathe. Never had he felt the punch of a woman's power like he did this one. It was like her energy had rolled across the beach and grabbed his soul, twisting it in knots until he didn't know whether to beg or run away. All he knew was that he had never in his life seen a woman so confident in her own power.

And it appeared they were staying in the same inn.

Not sure whether to be grateful or terrified, Ted waited

the requisite thirty minutes for the sunscreen to soak into his skin before venturing to the beach. He needed that time to calm his racing heart down as well, and push any untoward fantasies from his head. It wouldn't do to fantasize about another guest, he reminded himself. He was here for his work.

His one true love.

CHAPTER 3

*J*olie slammed the door to her room and raced to the bathroom, closing and locking that door before Mirra read her emotions and came after her. She just needed… a second. Or thousands of them. Her heart hammered in her chest and she gripped the sink, staring into the mirror. She looked slaphappy – giddy, almost – with wide eyes and pink-tinged cheeks. Bending, she turned the tap on and splashed some water across her face. It wasn't enough. Needing to cool down, Jolie stepped into the shower and ducked her head under the cool stream of water.

Her skin burned with need and her hand slipped to the straps of her bikini, untying them slowly and imagining the hands of her lover following their path over her body. Gasping, she pressed her hands to herself, once, twice, and finally offered herself a quick release of the tension that had shot through her the instant she'd caught sight of him.

Him.

The one she'd been waiting for all these years. Searching, Irma had said; Jolie was always searching. She'd be first to greet a new boat of sailors visiting, or happy to welcome any new tourists to town. It wasn't out of curiosity or boredom, oh no – it was because Irma was right. Jolie had been looking for her man, the one who'd been shown to her ages ago, the one she knew she'd feel the instant he was before her.

Grateful that she hadn't fallen into a puddle in the sand and had instead blown him a cheeky kiss before bolting inside, Jolie braced her arms against the shower wall and let the water run over her, soothing her skin. She took a few deep breaths to calm her scrambled thoughts.

It had been the oracle who'd shown her. Rarely did Jolie keep secrets from Mirra, but they'd kept their readings private from each other. It was a tradition of her people: The oracle provided a reading upon a child's birth and on their sixteenth birthday. Jolie remembered that day vividly.

It had been one of their biannual trips deep into the ocean to visit her mother's family. Though Mirra and Jolie were technically considered half-breeds because their father was human, they were always welcomed with open arms. In a society that was slowly dying off, babies were a reason to celebrate.

The oracle had swum with her, taking her deep inside an underground cavern where her magick would be hidden. Only then did the oracle close her eyes and project her reading on Jolie. The reading, presented in images in Jolie's mind instead of words, had seared into her memory.

She'd seen babies, many of them, and herself laughing with a man. A bridge, the oracle had kept flashing at her, until Jolie realized that part of her destiny was to be a bridge between their two kinds. It wasn't just about love – not for Jolie, at least. It was also about bringing understanding, acceptance, and growth to the merfolk who so desperately needed it. For centuries they'd been hunted, and as their numbers grew lower, a new choice was upon them: Bring humans into their fold or perish. It seemed the oracle wanted her family to work on it – as they were of both land and sea – and with that, her fate had been sealed.

But the man – oh, she'd only seen him for a second in the vision, but he'd also been imprinted in her mind. Not to mention how happy she'd looked.

She'd searched ever since, for ten years now, and was beginning to think the oracle had been wrong about her. Maybe she'd confused the reading because of Jolie's human blood?

But one look at Dr. Theodore Macalister had told her everything she needed to know.

And for that, she needed to bring out the big guns. Straightening, Jolie turned off the water and dried off, then wrapped her long hair into a towel and padded naked to her closet to examine her first line of attack – her wardrobe. She'd learned a lot about men over the years, and one thing she knew was that they loved a woman who showcased herself well. Biting her lip, she pawed through racks of dresses until she found something short, tight, and red. Red was a good color for her, and she knew for a fact it got men's pulses racing – she could feel their hearts start pounding from across the room.

Jolie pulled the dress over her head and shimmied it down her body inch by inch. She decided to forego any undergarments and let her body do the talking. She didn't expect it would be long before Dr. Macalister would be taking it off of her anyway, so why bother with underwear?

Humming to herself, she approached her makeup bag, then stepped back and examined her face in the mirror again. The shine was still on her, and Jolie decided the dress would be a statement on its own. After tucking some turquoise dangles in her ears, she unwrapped her hair and let it drop to her waist, knowing the sea breezes would tease it dry shortly. Humming, Jolie padded barefoot to the kitchen to dig up something to eat – as well as the gossip on their newest houseguest.

"So he's – oh my goddess, Jolie." Mirra cut off what she was saying when Jolie entered the kitchen and looked her sister up and down. "We already talked about the no-shagging rule. You look like sex on a stick."

"It's not my fault that red isn't your color, Mirra," Jolie quipped, and wandered to the cabinet to get a glass.

Done up in an open-air Tuscan style, the kitchen was the heart of the Laughing Mermaid. More often than not, Mirra, Jolie, and Irma could be found laughing or arguing at the long stretch of table that dominated the room. Guests were often invited to join; other times they dined alone.

"Mirra can wear red, Jolie. You're both blessed in the genes department. There isn't much that doesn't look good on either of you," Irma said, casting a look over her shoulder. She stood at the counter, stirring sauce in a pan. "Though I must say you do look extra alluring for our family dinner tonight. Any particular reason?"

"I just felt like wearing this dress. It's not like I put on makeup or heels or anything," Jolie pointed out, opening the fridge to pour herself a glass of prosecco.

"I'll take some," Mirra called.

"Get it yourself," Jolie countered, then jumped when Irma tugged her hair.

"Get your sister a glass of wine."

"Fine." Jolie glowered as she poured a glass for the beaming Mirra before settling herself in the chair at the end of the table. Reggae played lightly in the background, and through the open windows the sun made its nightly journey to meet the ocean. Mirra stuck her tongue out at Jolie, and despite herself, Jolie laughed.

"Punk."

"Brat," Mirra parried back.

"Ladies, I hope you get this out of your system, whatever it is, before our guest joins us for dinner."

"He is?" Jolie straightened, her voice taking on a high pitch. The other two women turned to look at her with curiosity. "I mean… that's nice. What's for dinner?"

"Caprese. And stuffed noodles with my red sauce." Irma returned to the stove, keeping one eye on her daughter and one on the food.

"Why are you so interested in our guest, Jolie? Been a slow month?" Mirra asked, then jumped when Jolie pinched her. Her eyes narrowed as she really looked at Jolie and then her face softened. That was Mirra – all heart.

"I don't know. It's just… something," Jolie admitted.

"I'm sorry. I shouldn't be poking at you. If you think it's something, I'll trust that."

"I don't know if it's something. I don't know what I think. It's just…"

"Something," Mirra finished, patting her hand.

"Yeah," Jolie said, gulping her prosecco, hoping the liquid would cool her burning throat.

"I don't think I've seen you like this before. It's like you're nervous. Why are you nervous? Men eat out of your hand."

"True, they do." Jolie saw no sense in lying. Making men fall for her had always come easy. The hard part was finding one she wanted to stick around.

"We have a rule," Irma reminded them.

"I know, I know, don't sleep with the guests."

"Um… I'm sorry to interrupt…"

A voice at the doorway sent shivers through her body and heat rushing to her cheeks. There was no way their guest hadn't just heard Irma. Closing her eyes, Jolie took one more sip of her drink before opening them and looking at the man who was her destiny.

He looked equally as poleaxed as she was. Well, that made two of them. At least it was a party now.

"Prosecco?" Jolie asked.

He nodded, his cheeks still bright red with embarrassment, and Jolie rushed to fill his drink and cover the awkward silence that filled the kitchen.

"Ted, I'd like you to meet Jolie and Mirra, my daughters."

"My pleasure," Ted said, offering his hand to each of them. Jolie held his a second too long, letting his energy pulse through her before looking up at him from under heavy lids.

"The pleasure is all mine."

"No seduction at the dinner table, Jolie. The man is already uncomfortable enough," Irma cut in, putting baskets of bread on the table and banishing any attempt that Jolie could have made toward redeeming herself.

She glared grumpily at Irma, ignored Mirra's giggle, and stuck her nose in her wine.

Maybe she'd find her answers there.

CHAPTER 4

"I must apologize," Ted said, holding up his hands. "I didn't bring anything for dinner. I know it's rude of me, but I don't have transportation yet."

"It's not a problem, Ted. But it's really nice of you to think of that." Jolie beamed up at him and enjoyed the pink that flushed his cheeks once again when he glanced at her and then away. The man did have the nicest green eyes, highlighted by the green canvas shirt he wore. His hair – light brown tinged with gold – was just long enough that she could run her hands through it, and broad shoulders hinted at strong arms and a lean build under his loose shirt. She wanted to undress him – preferably with her mouth. She licked her lips thinking about it. Ted caught his toe on the bench as he moved to sit down, and looked away from her again. Jolie could all but read his silent beratement of his clumsiness.

"I catch my foot on that all the time. It's why I choose the chair at the end of the table and not the bench," Jolie offered. Ted nodded, smiling a little in his embarrassment.

"Here's your prosecco." Mirra slid a blue glass in front of Ted, and he expressed his thanks. He looked around the kitchen, his eyes missing nothing, and blinked at the three women. Jolie could easily see his awkwardness at finding himself cozied up in their kitchen. She often forgot the impact the three of them had on men.

"Everything okay, Ted?" Jolie purred, and Ted jumped at being addressed.

"Ah." Ted cleared his throat and then took a sip. "Yes, I'm fine. I just can't decide what's more intoxicating – the scents coming from the oven or being in this space with the three of you at once. If I didn't know better, I'd say I'd landed in a Greek myth where the goddesses serve decadent meals and men bow to their whims."

Well, well, well, Jolie thought, surprised at Dr. Macalister's depths, and that he had the confidence to voice his thoughts even though the faint blush on his cheeks still gave away his nervousness. She hadn't expected to find him cute or endearing, and this was adding new layers to the image she'd built in her head over the years.

"Well, isn't that sweet of you, Ted." Mirra beamed at him and passed him the basket of fresh-baked bread that Irma had just placed on the table. "Our mother was just reminding us how blessed we are in the genes department."

"She's not wrong. The three of you are some of the most beautiful women I've ever seen. And I live in a city chock-full of stunning women."

Jolie was miffed to think of Ted eyeing up other women, not to mention the fact that he'd included her sister and mother in his compliments. Not that she didn't think they were beautiful, because of course they were. But she wanted his attention on *her*, damn it.

"And what city is that?"

"I'm in Boston," Ted said, glancing at Jolie and then sliding his eyes away. It was like he couldn't hold her gaze, Jolie thought, and narrowed her eyes at him. Every time he looked at her, he quickly moved on, never hovering for too long. She wondered why. Did he feel the same things she was feeling?

"I've heard great things about Boston. What's your favorite thing about the city?" Mirra asked, spreading butter on a slice of bread she pulled from the basket.

"Hmm, it's hard to name just one thing. But I think it's being able to walk along the Charles River or the waterfront. I love being near water. It gives me time to think and to decompress after a long day. I need the outside time to recharge. Not every city can offer me green space and proximity to water."

"What do you need to decompress from?" Jolie asked, then looked up when Irma nudged her. "What?"

"It's rude to ask such intimate questions. You've just met him."

"It's not rude if he brought it up, is it?" Jolie turned to Ted and demanded, "Am I being rude?"

Ted flushed again under her stare. "Ah, well, no, I don't mind answering the question. I get, well, I guess I get stressed from being 'on' all day. Or talking all day. I tend to be a bit of a loner, so I need to recharge my emotional batteries by being alone in nature for a while."

"That makes sense. It's my favorite part about being in the ocean," Jolie said, sipping her wine and smiling to herself when his gaze darted away from her again. Oh yes, the man was definitely affected by her. "Nobody can reach me. No cell phones, no computers. No people to bother me."

"I think that's part of why I'm so drawn to water. That and mermaids, of course," Ted said – then looked up when everyone in the room paused what they were doing and stared at him. "Um… hmm. I suppose I should expand on that?"

"Please do," Jolie said, narrowing her eyes a bit as she studied him.

"Well, it's part of what I do, you see."

"You're a mermaid doctor?" Irma asked.

Ted laughed – a real laugh this time, not an embarrassed chuckle – and the timbre of it made heat roll through Jolie's stomach.

"I should only be so lucky. No, I'm a literature professor, with a more specific focus on mythology. And a particular area of focus for me is mermaid mythology. I've always been drawn to it. That's why I chose Siren Island – because of the rich history of mermaid myths. In truth, I needed a vacation, but I thought I might as well combine it with two of the things I love – the ocean and mermaids. Finding your guesthouse was an added bonus."

"Well, we do love all things mermaid," Irma agreed, bending to pull a steaming dish of stuffed shells from the oven and placing it on the counter. "I'm sure any one of us would be happy to help you in your research."

"Really? That'd be fantastic, actually. There wasn't much I could find on the internet in the way of documentation or local narratives. I'd certainly appreciate it if you could point me in the right direction of anyone with historical knowledge of the legends here."

"You're looking at one of them. Well, three of them, actually." Mirra laughed as Ted's face brightened, and she nodded to her mother. "Irma is a good resource."

"Is she?" Ted turned and sized up Irma again – and for the first time in her life, Jolie found herself jealous of her mother. "Are you?"

"I am. But Jolie's just as handy a resource. Perhaps you can take him to town tomorrow to sort out his transportation? Then maybe take him by Prince's house and he could have a chat."

"A chat? You'll be there all day. The man never stops talking."

"I don't mind. It's fascinating learning from others. I'm quite content to sit and listen all day if that's what it takes."

"What do you hope to learn about the mermaids while you're here?" Mirra asked.

"Well, really I'm just fascinated by how so many cultures have stories of mermaids, and how closely the stories often line up. These myths come from centuries ago when there was no way to exchange the stories, so I find it very interesting that similar characteristics have developed in legends across the world."

"Do you believe that mermaids could be real?" Jolie asked. Irma went still at the counter.

"I would be the luckiest man on earth if I discovered they were real," Ted said, and smiled when Irma brought a plate over to him.

"What would you do with that information if you did find them?" Jolie asked.

"If I actually found evidence that mermaids were real? Hmm, that's a tough question," Ted mused. He had waited to take a bite of his dinner until Irma had joined them at the table; now he added, "This is delicious."

"Thank you," Irma said. "Go on."

"If I found out they were truly real, I think I could die a happy man. But I'd hope I could also study them and learn about them."

"Study them – like in a lab?"

"No! Goodness, no. Never. That would be the other piece of it. I'd want them protected and not exploited. So perhaps it would just be a private win for me, and I could maybe verify some truths about the mythology of mermaids? Honestly, I just don't know. I suspect I'd have an endless number of questions, and then I'd likely write a paper about it."

Jolie froze at his words. "A paper?"

"Sure. I mean, I couldn't reveal my sources without exposing the mermaids, but I might be able to add some correlation or layers to past myths. It's really fascinating, actually. I'm sure I'd figure out the angle eventually. After I got over the sheer joy of seeing a mermaid, that is."

"What makes you think a mermaid would agree to tell you her story?" Jolie speared her fork into a stuffed shell, torn between her feelings for Ted and his desire to learn more about their kind.

"I don't. I truly don't think she would tell me her story. Why would she? If they *are* real, they have no reason to trust humans, based on the stories I've read. And vice versa, I suppose. Humans haven't always fared well at the hands of sirens, either."

"For good reason," Mirra murmured, but snapped her mouth shut when Jolie shot her a look.

"You're absolutely right, Mirra. For good reason. If mermaids are real, I think they're smart to stay hidden."

"And yet you'd write a paper on them."

"I'd write a paper on the *legends* of them, and might be able to add some new insights that haven't been uncovered before." Ted's face lit up as he talked – he was clearly passionate about the subject – and Jolie wanted him to look at her like that too.

"Well, we're happy to have you here. I'm certain we'll be able to point you in the right direction for your research. Is there anything else you'd like to do with your time here? We can help with renting boats and activities like that as well," Irma said, smoothly shifting the conversation.

"I think I'll be fine so long as I can arrange transportation. I'm fairly good at finding my way around on my own. I'm used to it."

"No wife back home missing you?" Jolie asked; then it was her turn to clamp her mouth shut when her sister shot her a look.

"Oh, um, no. I'm single. Much to my parents' chagrin." Ted smiled easily, and the moment passed.

"Don't I know it," Irma said, looking at both her daughters.

"We have time yet, Mother," Mirra said, while Jolie dropped her eyes to her plate and found her own cheeks burning. It wasn't like her to feel shy or uncomfortable around a man. This… this was different. It all felt outside her comfort zone. Was this what love was?

"You have all the time in the world. You know I'll never push anyone on you." Irma smiled at them both. "I think it's important you find your own way."

"She says that now, but I bet in five years she gets a lot more pushy," Jolie said, and smiled when Ted let out another robust laugh. It warmed her to know she'd made him laugh, and she wanted to do it again.

"I might. We'll see. Jolie, can you take Ted to town tomorrow?"

"I can. Do you want to rent a scooter or a truck? I'd recommend a truck, but I'm not sure of your budget."

"A truck would be perfect. I imagine there are a few off-road spots here that'll be tricky for a scooter."

"Great; it's a date." Jolie almost slapped a hand over her mouth.

"Right," Ted said, nodding and not meeting her eyes. "I'll plan for it."

At that, Jolie gave up and downed her glass of wine. She'd embarrassed herself enough for one evening.

CHAPTER 5

*T*ed had excused himself after dinner, claiming tiredness from his travels – but in truth, he was revved. It was like his blood was humming underneath his skin and he wasn't sure what to do about it. If it hadn't been night, he would have jumped in the ocean and swum until the anxious feeling dissipated and he was once more at peace.

God, he'd been such an idiot at dinner. Groaning, Ted poured himself a glass of wine from the bottle that had been stocked in the room, and dropped into the chair on the balcony. The moon, halfway through its monthly turn, shed enough light to sprinkle diamonds across the dark water. Ted wiped a hand over his face and took a slug of the wine before propping his feet on the wall of the balcony and letting his head fall back to look up at the stars.

He'd just *had* to talk about the mermaids.

Aside from his students, nobody in his life could really understand his fascination with mythology – specifically mermaid mythology. He'd learned to change the subject at dinner parties after going on one too many tangents about some historical tidbit he'd recently uncovered in his research. Now, he typically managed his social anxiety by being the one to ask questions of everyone else. One thing he'd learned quickly was that people loved to talk about themselves. So long as he asked the right questions, remained interested, and didn't make an ass of himself, he could generally leave most social gatherings feeling accomplished.

Tonight though, he'd been overwhelmed. He had even caught himself stumbling over his words a few times – falling back into a slight stuttering habit he'd grown out of as a kid – and had even tripped over the table. Sighing, he took another sip of his wine and let the sound of the waves soothe him. It wasn't a big deal, he reminded himself. The women had been more than gracious and had seemed interested in his conversation. These were his people, Ted thought. There was no way they could run a mermaid-themed guesthouse without loving them and the stories about them. He hadn't made all that much of a fool of himself. The anxiety kicking in his stomach retreated a bit, and he took a few deep breaths to calm himself before letting his mind settle where it really wanted to.

On Jolie.

He hadn't even been able to look at her full-on – at least, not for long. It was like staring at the sun. Just the sight of her when he'd walked into the kitchen, not to mention overhearing the comment about sex, had sent all of his senses into overdrive. He'd never met a more potent woman in his life and Ted had shocked himself by how much he wanted to touch her.

Hell, to *touch* her? Kiss her. Talk to her. Be near her. It was as if Irma and Mirra had faded into the shadows, and Jolie had been this bright ball of energy pulling him to her. It had taken everything in his willpower to not crawl to her at the table and beg her to bestow a few words of kindness upon him. Like a pauper to a queen or an errand boy to a goddess, Ted would submit himself to her will if she'd only give him a chance.

Which she wouldn't, Ted reminded himself, and took another sip of his wine. It was his experience that women like Jolie did not go for men like Ted. Hell, women like Jolie didn't even *notice* men like Ted. His whole life he'd been ignored or steamrolled by women who looked like Jolie. When they did pay attention to him – like his graduate students – it was because they wanted something.

Jolie, in all her beauty and confidence, was quite simply terrifying to Ted. So he would do what he always did in situations like this – refuse to read into anything and keep his distance. He'd already overheard their rule about not sleeping with guests, and there was no way he was interested in getting on Irma's bad side. Really, then, the choice – he laughed and shook his head at himself; like he had an actual choice. But even if he'd had one, it was out of his hands. Ted was a rule follower and it wouldn't do to fall into the bad graces of any of these women. The women of the Laughing Mermaid were a formidable lot. Ted planned to admire them from afar and do his best to not break any of their rules.

An image of Jolie laughing flashed into his mind. The

breath had left his body and he'd been dead in the water the minute he'd seen her smile. But Jolie laughing? It was the first time Ted had believed goddesses to be real. No mortal human could embody such beauty. If she'd let him, he would photograph her. Just one picture – Jolie laughing – that he could take home and pin to the corkboard above his desk. When the days were long and cold in the dead of winter of Boston, he'd look at the photo and find all the warmth he needed.

CHAPTER 6

"Go easy on him, Jolie. He's shy," Mirra advised the next morning as she lay on Jolie's bed and studied her sister, who was standing in front of her closet.

"He's not that shy. He called us goddesses last night."

"And then blushed immediately after."

"I know. Isn't he darling?" Jolie laughed and whirled, beaming at Mirra – who looked at her and sighed.

"Jolie. He's a guest."

"Yes, yes, I know the rules."

"He's not yours to play with. Find someone else."

"I will make my own decisions, thank you very much, sister of mine." Jolie tied the halter straps of her breezy turquoise dress around her neck and dropped a layered necklace with brilliant orange beads over her head. Shaking her hair out, she let it tumble to her waist and grabbed her oversized white sunglasses. "How do I look?"

"Stunning. As usual. Which shouldn't matter when you're driving a guest on an errand."

"It's important to take pride in how you look, Mirra. Otherwise, how do you show your confidence?"

"Oh, please. You are the least insecure person I know. Your picture is next to the definition of self-confidence in the dictionary. I have never seen you awkward or uncomfortable in any situation. In fact, you gaining more confidence is… scary. You'd terrorize the world. No, Jolie, more confidence is not what you need. But what you do need to do is tell me what's going on with you."

"Nothing's going on with me," Jolie said, slinging her woven mochila bag over her shoulder.

"A liar you are not."

"Fine – there is something going on. I'm just not ready to talk about it," Jolie admitted, turning to meet Mirra's eyes. "Give me some time, okay?"

"Is there anything I can do? Do you need me?" Mirra asked, concern crossing her pretty face. Jolie sighed. Even though they often butted heads as sisters, they were and always would be best friends. It felt weird to not discuss this with her, but until Jolie could wrap her head around her own feelings upon seeing Ted and realizing he was her destiny, she wasn't ready to open up.

"No, I'm okay. I promise that when I'm ready to talk, I'll come to you. You know I always do."

"I love you, Jolie. Just… be careful with Ted, okay? I like him."

"I like him too. I'll be on my best behavior."

"That's what scares me."

"Don't be jealous that I've got better game than you," Jolie said, laughing as she left her room to meet Ted out front. A flutter of nerves raced through her, stopping her in her tracks. It was such an unusual sensation, she realized, to be nervous about seeing a man. But this one – well, this one mattered.

"Good morning, Jolie," Ted said when she stepped outside. He was leaning against a palm tree; aviator glasses shaded his eyes, and a well-worn leather backpack hung over one broad shoulder. Today he wore loose board shorts and a faded blue t-shirt that showed more of his muscles. He didn't spend *all* his time with his head buried in books, Jolie thought as she ran her eyes over his muscular arms. "Don't you look lovely this morning?"

"Thank you." Jolie beamed at him and slid her sunglasses on to hide just how much the compliment delighted her. "And you look well-rested and settled in. Did you sleep okay?"

"Just fine, thank you. The room is great and after another glass of the wine you stocked, I was out like a light."

"That's good to hear. Would you like me to take you on a little tour of the island first to help you get acclimated, or do you want to pick up your truck right away?"

"Um… well, a tour would be nice. And perhaps an introduction to the man you mentioned last night? Or if I could have his phone number, I can arrange all that. No need to bother you."

"It's no bother. Tour it is." Jolie motioned to the same pickup truck Irma had used the day before to pick Ted up. He paused for a moment, looking back at the house and then to the truck. Jolie asked, "Did you forget something?"

"Is this your only car?"

"It is."

"Well, then, I couldn't possibly take up your time. What if they need it?"

"They'll call me if they do. I don't think they had plans to go to town today, though – I already have my list of what to get from the shops for them."

"Oh. Well, if you're sure…"

"You're very sweet, Ted." Jolie flashed him a grin and delight slid through her when his cheeks went pink again. A few days in the sun and she wouldn't be able to notice his blush anymore. "But we're used to navigating around having one car. And Mirra has a scooter if there's a need for anything."

"Ah, okay. Then if you're sure I'm not imposing, I'd love a tour." Ted put his pack in the back of the truck after pulling a little camera from the front pocket, and settled himself in the front seat. Jolie smiled to herself as she got behind the wheel. It was nice to know he was also considerate. It was a good quality to have in a man.

Her life partner.

Nerves flitted through her again. Jolie stalled the truck when she shifted into first, and she stared at the dashboard, her mouth hanging open.

"I can't believe this!"

"It's okay. I'm not great at driving stick myself."

"I've been driving a stick shift since I was twelve. I can't tell you the last time I stalled the truck," Jolie said. She huffed out a laugh, shaking her head at her incompetence, then forced herself to focus and get the truck moving.

"Twelve, huh? That's a little young to be driving."

"Ah, well, island life is a little more relaxed on these

things. I can't say I was legally driving at that time, but I learned enough to get around. If there had been an emergency, I could have gotten someone to the doctor if I'd needed to."

"I never thought about that. No ambulance services here, I suppose?"

"There are. But sometimes the quickest way is to get to the hospital yourself."

"I can see that. Kind of like where I grew up. We lived in a more rural part of Vermont. You had to be much more self-sufficient there; the nearest hospital was a good forty-five minutes away."

"Exactly. You learn to make do on an island. And learn basic skills. Like driving a stick shift." Jolie shook her head and laughed at herself once more, sliding a glance at Ted to see him studying her, his mouth hanging slightly open. Good, she thought. He wasn't impervious to her.

"I'm just happy I have an automatic back home."

"I must have been distracted by you," Jolie said, widening her smile and glancing at him again. Testing the waters, she thought.

"Oh, I'm sorry," Ted said automatically. "You're right – I shouldn't have been talking when you were driving. I'll be quiet."

"What? No, that's not what I meant." Jolie blew out a breath. Okay, that had crashed and burned. "Just you know… handsome man and all."

"Oh."

The silence drew out until Jolie's eyes widened and her hands clenched on the steering wheel. 'Oh'? Was that all the man could say? She'd opened the way for flirtation and… crickets.

"So, this is the road to the downtown, but if we go left here there's a mermaid statue over by the cliffs you might like to see."

"I'd love to, thank you. Is there a historical significance to the statue?"

"There is, actually. I can tell you the story when we get there. Have you read much about how Siren Island got its name?" Jolie steered the conversation back to Ted's comfort zone, grateful they weren't sitting in silence anymore, and mentally kicked herself. How had she bungled that so badly? Usually she was an expert at flirtatious banter, but her one gentle attempt had bombed. Taking a deep breath, she chattered on about points of interest they passed as her brain whirled, trying to think how to handle things next.

She'd obviously made Ted uncomfortable. It bothered her to think that, but there was really no way around it. Usually, Jolie would dial up the heat at this point. But if even a single flirty comment flustered him, it wouldn't be kind of her to make him more uncomfortable. Instead, she kept the conversation light, pointing out new developments on the island and various sights he could go visit when he had his own transportation.

"Oh, I see the statue!" Ted laughed – his real laugh, not his embarrassed one – and she found herself laughing with him. She'd never seen a grown man so enchanted by mermaids before.

"Yes, it's cool, isn't it?"

"I'll say. The artist did lovely work."

"I'll get us closer," Jolie promised, and turned down a lane concealed by overgrown bush. The truck rattled its way down a dirt road with two large ruts in the middle. Slowing to a crawl, Jolie brought the truck as close as she could without blowing a tire out, and parked.

Ted stepped away from the truck. "She's beautiful," he breathed, his camera in hand, shooting photo after photo.

"You should see her when the sun sets."

"Oh, I can imagine it's breathtaking. The gorgeous lines of her body and down through her tail? With the sun framing her from behind? Oh yeah, she's a knock-out. What a lovely rendering," Ted gushed. He moved forward, then cursed as he stubbed his toe against a craggy rock that jutted from the sand.

"Careful. There are loads of little prickly plants as well. Desert island and all," Jolie said, picking her way over the rocks toward the cliff where the mermaid statue was.

"I know. I just get caught up sometimes and forget my surroundings," Ted said, running a hand through his hair.

I wish he'd get caught up in me, Jolie thought, but bit her tongue as she followed Ted to the base of the cliff so they could both gaze up at the beautiful statue above.

"Her name is Irmine. And she waits here, protecting the fishermen and grieving her lover."

"Is that so? I can see it in her face."

"Mermaids know," Jolie said, forcing herself not to turn and look at Ted and say, 'Don't you see? I'm right here.' Instead, she crouched and picked up a small shell with a hole in the middle.

"They know what?"

"Their destiny. When one man is meant for them versus all the others they toy with."

"How do they know?"

"The oracle tells them."

"They have an oracle? Really? That's something I haven't heard before. At least in mermaid myths. Can you tell me more?" Ted asked, excitement lacing his words.

"Of course. Let's settle in and I'll tell you the story of young Nalachi." Jolie pointed to a smooth rock with enough room for the two of them to sit, tucked under the shade of a scraggly tree, its branches growing sideways in the wind.

"I can't wait. Can I record you?" Ted asked, pulling a little recorder from his pack, and Jolie laughed.

"Of course."

CHAPTER 7

"*I*f you can imagine, this island was just a small fishing village years ago. Trade routes were established between other islands, but aside from those, this place was left largely undisturbed."

Ted nodded, silently encouraging her to continue.

"As time went on and fisherman got used to traversing the routes to other islands, trade picked up and there was more travel. Which in turn meant more people on the water. Many of whom reported seeing... beings in the water. Usually late at night."

"Beings."

"Yes. Half-woman, half-fish. The locals whispered of it, but many questioned what they saw, or were too frightened to speak of it much. Still, the stories filtered through the villages. One young fisherman in particular was quite interested in the stories; he would spend long hours at sea at night, his eyes trained on the horizon, hoping to find one of these woman-fish creatures."

"As I would be," Ted murmured. Jolie bit back a smile,

but kept her eyes on a gull swooping over the mermaid statue on the cliff.

"One night they had a big festival, and our fisherman, Nalachi – the most handsome lad in the village, by the way – was there to help his ailing mother serve food. His mother hoped he'd find a pretty village maiden to settle down with. But Nalachi was a dreamer. He looked to the horizon more often than not, as if he were waiting for something."

Jolie knew that feeling, and now she identified more deeply than ever with Nalachi's story.

"Did he take off on a grand adventure?" Ted asked, his shoulder casually brushing hers.

Jolie's senses seemed to zero in on the spot where his arm had touched hers. "Ah, yes." Jolie cleared her throat. "But not yet. That night at the festival, a young woman appeared as if from nowhere. Nalachi's heart stopped when his eyes landed on the fair maiden, and he knew love instantly. His gaze followed her as she danced around the fire, her laughter a song on the wind, and more than one man was entranced by her charm. But with one look from Nalachi, the rest faded away and he knew."

"Did he approach her?"

"He did. He learned her name was Irmine, and together they danced through the evening – the fire roaring around them, sweat dripping down their bodies, until all they heard was the primal beat of the drum." Jolie crossed her legs uncomfortably, feeling the pull of Ted deep in her core, wanting him to recognize her as young Nalachi had Irmine. "She slipped away when he went to bring them water and Nalachi pursued her until he found her at the cliff's edge."

"Up there?" Ted pointed to the statue.

"Yes, way out on the cliffs. She insisted she must go, but Nalachi begged her to stay – or, at the very least, to leave something of hers. She gave him a shell necklace, a passionate kiss, and told him to listen for her song. He blinked, and then she was gone."

"Ah. Tough for the young man."

"That it was. Despondent, Nalachi took to the water each day, searching for boats he didn't recognize and listening for a song. She'd sung it to him right before she disappeared, you see."

"What's the song?"

"Where the starlight kisses the sea, this is where you'll find me. It won't be so long, for in your heart is my song," Jolie sang – softly, because she didn't want the full power of her voice to entrance Ted. It was important to her that he choose her of his own accord and not because of any enchantments. A siren's voice was one of her biggest magicks, and it was best to tread carefully when using it. Even at low power, Jolie could see Ted was touched.

"That's beautiful. I love the imagery," Ted said softly, and Jolie wondered if he realized that he'd picked up her hand. She allowed him to hold it for a moment longer as its warmth radiated up her palm and to her heart, then gently disengaged. She bit back a smile as he looked down in shock at his hand and then hers, his cheeks flaming that delicious pink color again. "I'm sorry. It appears I got caught up in the story. That happens sometimes. I have a tendency to dream."

"There's nothing wrong with being a dreamer."

"So, Irmine has sung for Nalachi and left him a token of her affection. Do they meet again? Or is she always up there searching?" Ted squinted his eyes at the cliffs. "Wait – wouldn't it be Nalachi searching for her?"

"Good question, Dr. Macalister," Jolie said with a smile. "Not everyone catches that. So, Nalachi heads to the water each night until, a month later, he's shocked to find pretty Irmine dancing over the cliffs to him. It was in that moment his heart was fully lost, for she sang for him. And together, they were lost to each other, and gave each other their love under the light of the full moon."

"I hope they had a blanket to lie on," Ted said, squinting his eyes at the craggy volcanic rock that lined the cliff's edge.

Jolie shocked herself by snorting, and then covered her face with her hand and laughed even harder. "I can't believe I just snorted." She wiped a tear from her eye.

"I can't believe you did either." Ted grinned at her, then shrugged. "I'm practical to a fault at times. It just looks like it might be an uncomfortable spot for lovemaking."

"There's a sandy beach on the other side," Jolie said, and Ted nodded in understanding.

"Phew. Now that the logistics of that are worked out – continue?"

"Oh yes, phew, now that we're certain our young lovers have made a comfortable bed for themselves, we may continue." Jolie threw her head back and laughed again. "You're something else, Dr. Macalister."

"I can get a little stuck on details."

"Not a problem. After our young lovers worshipped each other for the evening, Nalachi awoke alone as the sun cracked the horizon."

"Ah, been there, done that. It's not fun."

"I can't imagine a woman leaving you behind," Jolie said, turning to look at Ted. His nearness excited her, and she found herself licking her lips, her eyes on his, wanting a taste.

"Oh, imagine it. It was more the norm than not. I guess I wasn't exciting enough for the ladies."

"I highly doubt that," Jolie purred, and Ted's shoulders tensed. Realizing she was making him uncomfortable, Jolie did something she rarely did – she backed off. "But yes, Nalachi was left alone on the beach, his heart in his hands. Yet a month later, after moping his way along the cliffs each night, Irmine returned to him for another evening of love."

"Hmm – on the moon cycle?"

"Correct. And it didn't take long for Nalachi to realize she was visiting him at the full moon. So he devised a plan to keep her with him. He was lovesick with missing her, you see – when she was gone, he'd barely eat, and would take to the ocean for hours at a time. It was getting so bad that he was determined to stop her from leaving the next time she visited."

"He – he restrained her?"

"He did. And when light returned the next morning, he learned her secret."

"He killed her."

"Oh! No, he didn't kill her." Jolie touched his hand, as Ted looked genuinely upset. "No – she had turned mermaid and was dying from being out of the water, so he carried her in and let her go. Nalachi knew that if he really loved her, he had to set her free."

"Did Irmine ever return to him? I wonder if she was angry."

"She did return. Unfortunately, Nalachi had been called away to work on a new trade vessel between islands; he was away every full moon for the next six months. Irmine was convinced he didn't love her as he'd said."

"Ouch."

"'Ouch' is right. Especially as she was carrying his children."

"Really? What is the birth cycle for a mermaid? Is there any knowledge on that? Are the babies born in water or on land? Do they have gills if they're born in water? I wonder how it all works." Ted began patting his pockets for a notebook.

"Focus, Theodore," Jolie said, snapping her fingers in front of his nose. "Babies are always a blessing in the mermaid world. But some cast judgment when a baby has a human parent."

"But… aren't mermaids half human?"

"They were a long time ago, but they don't need humans to procreate anymore. Their species evolved."

"Ah," Ted said, nodding as though he really believed everything she said.

"Irmine's father was not happy that she had chosen a human for the father of her babies. He kept her away after that, determined to save her from what he believed were destructive humans. But in doing so, he actually caused the tragic end to this love story."

"Oh my. Controlling parents are tricky."

"They can be, I've heard."

"Go on," Ted gestured.

"Finally, after many months, Nalachi made it home for a full moon. He raced to the shoreline, hoping to see Irmine. Ignoring the clouds on the horizon, which any sailor would know meant heavy storms were coming, Nalachi rowed himself out, hoping he would find the one woman whose song he still carried in his heart. But he was so focused on looking at the horizon that he missed the signs of a reef and cracked his hull on it. Nalachi tried to decide whether he should swim for land, but then the storm hit. Clinging to his boat, with his last breaths he began to sing the song his love had given him."

"Oh no. Did she come for him? Please tell me she did."

"She did. That's our Irmine. A strong woman who defied her father's wishes and rushed with her daughters to save the man she loved. Unfortunately, she found him as his soul left him, and he was too far gone for her magick to save him. He smiled for her, whispering his love.

"She took his soul then and forged it into a pearl to wear on a necklace. It is said that she still sings each night to warn the sailors away from danger; for those who are lost at sea, she turns their souls into pearls of the sea – singing even louder so their lovers across the water will know she's caring for them in the afterlife."

"How horribly tragic – yet deeply romantic."

"She knew she was loved, though. It would be horrible, wouldn't it? To think you were never loved?"

"I can understand that," Ted said, his voice soft as he looked up at the statue.

"She's the mother of the sea now. From here, she sings her songs of love and protection." Jolie gestured to the statue once more, her heart aching for Irmine. Jolie wanted to know the love she had known.

It was written in her blood, after all.

CHAPTER 8

*J*olie followed Ted to the cliffs while he peppered her with questions, stopping every so often to clarify an issue or to make a note into the recorder he carried with him. He was nerdy to the point that most people might find him boring, but the more questions he asked, the more Jolie found herself entranced by him.

It wasn't any one thing in particular, she realized, as she watched him photograph and – was he really measuring the statue with a pocket tape measure? Biting back a smile, she perched herself on a rock and wound her hair up on top of her head to keep the breezes from blowing it across her face. Ted had an inquisitive mind, a non-judgmental attitude, and a body with enough muscles to make Jolie lick her lips again. She'd never been too interested in the brainy type, preferring brawn and good looks over the placid book-readers. Yet here she was, mooning after a man who was a delicious combination of both. She wondered if he had any idea how delectable he was.

"Jolie?"

"I'm sorry, what was that?" Jolie realized he'd been speaking to her again.

"I asked if you were ready to leave. I think I have all the documentation I need for now. I can come back if I have more questions."

"Sure, I'm happy to leave."

Following her down the cliff path back to where the truck was parked, Ted asked, "Do you know the artist who made the statue?"

"No. It just appeared."

Jolie jolted as Ted stumbled into her, and his arm automatically came around her waist, pulling her close to keep her from pitching forward down the rocky path.

"Are you okay?" he asked, his breath warm at her ear.

Jolie's insides went liquid. "Yes, I'm fine," she said. Then, testing him, she turned her head so that her mouth wasn't far from his. Instantly, Ted released her, easing back.

"I can be pretty clumsy. My sister always teased me about it growing up. Head in the clouds, I guess. I was just surprised that a massive statue like that could appear overnight with nobody the wiser. How can that be?"

"Magick." Jolie shrugged a shoulder as they approached the truck. Stopping at the driver's side door, she looked at him across the hood.

"Magick. Really? You believe that?"

"I do."

"Why?"

"Why not?"

"Why not believe in magick? I guess for probably a million scientific reasons I can't begin to name."

"And yet you're here chasing mermaids." Jolie kept her tone light as she eased herself into the car, pushing back the annoyance at his questions. She wanted him to believe, damn it.

"I suppose that's true," Ted laughed, pulling his seatbelt on with a click. His face lit up when he was talking about something he was passionate about, and Jolie had to force herself to keep her eyes on the road and not on him. "I guess it's easier for me to believe in myths and stories passed down through the centuries than in actual magick."

"Myths are their own magick, no? Stories passed from mouth to mouth through the years, incantations and rituals shoring up the words, so the truths shine on."

"Yes, I suppose. But I guess it's a bit more difficult for me to believe that suddenly – POOF! – a statue appeared on the cliffs from thin air."

"I can understand why that's hard to believe. Nevertheless, it's the truth," Jolie said, testing him to see if he would talk down to her.

"Noted." Ted smiled at her and the tension eased from Jolie's shoulders. While she didn't think he completely accepted her explanation for how the statue had arrived on the cliffs, at the very least he was willing to accept that *she* believed it. That was an important distinction in her mind.

"I think you'll find your time here very enlightening," Jolie said, pulling the truck into a small lane that led to a large whitewashed villa by the water.

"It already has been. I hope by the end of my stay I'll have learned many new things."

"First stop, let's get you some wheels."

"Here?" Ted craned his neck to look around, but saw no car.

"Yes, here. Come with me." Jolie smiled and slipped from the truck, then approached the garage and keyed in a code. When the door opened, a dusty island pickup truck, much like the one they'd just been riding in, sat in the garage.

"I was expecting something like a Porsche with this fancy villa," Ted laughed.

"Ah, see, here's a simple truth about cars and living in humidity and near saltwater: Everything corrodes. Our island mechanics are more likely to have parts for a basic island truck than they will for a high-end car. When inevitably your fancy Porsche breaks, it may be weeks before a part can be shipped in to fix it. So, we stick to simple cars that are easy to care for. It's annoying that cars wear down so quickly here. But, why bother spending the money on something that will just deteriorate?"

"No flashy convertible for you? Somehow I pictured you with your hair blowing behind you on a curvy cliff road," Ted said – then caught himself as he realized he was being fanciful.

"In this heat? Are you crazy? No, thank you. I'll take the shade and air conditioning of my truck."

"Ah, there goes the romance of that image," Ted said with a laugh.

"Oh, there are many romantic images to be found on-island," Jolie replied. "Just not when you're fried pink from the sun and have sweat pooling under your butt because you insisted on taking the top off your convertible."

"Chafing." Ted sighed and shook his head.

At his quip, Jolie shocked herself by snorting again. Where was her dignity? "I can't believe I snorted again! That's not fair. I'm supposed to be alluring and confident." Jolie stamped her foot, indignant that the snort was ruining her carefully crafted image.

"Thank god you did. You'd be scary if you didn't have some flaws. And it's not even a flaw, it's cute," Ted said absentmindedly while he checked the truck over. He opened the driver's door and popped the hood, pulling a bandana from his pocket as he reached for the oil stick.

"Wait, here," Jolie said, her mind still stuck on the fact that he thought she was cute. "There's a garage rag."

"Thanks," Ted said. He checked the oil, his head in another place, and she wondered if he even realized how easily he'd complimented her. But at the same time, he seemed completely unruffled by her presence.

Jolie leaned against the truck, biting a nail, as she watched Ted bury his head in the engine. Her mother would call this a lesson in humility, she supposed. She'd gotten used to men all but crawling to her; having one essentially treat her like a cute kid sister was not something she was even remotely accustomed to.

Being uncomfortable is how you grow.

Jolie rolled her eyes at her mother's voice in her head. The woman was right, of course, but that didn't mean Jolie had to like it. She sighed, stepping away from the truck as

Ted slammed the hood. She supposed nothing good in life came easily.

"Everything looks good, though I'd like to top off the oil; it's getting a bit low. Is there a shop in town where I can pick some up?"

"Sure, I can lead you there."

"Also, if you could –" Ted cut himself off and shook his head, laughing a little at himself. "I'm sorry. I know you're not my personal tour guide and I'm sure you have a life outside of showing me all over the island."

"I am but your humble servant," Jolie said with a bow. She warmed inside when he laughed at her.

"You're being very kind. But I'm sure this is above and beyond your duties."

"It's slow season, so we have more time to be available to our guests. Plus, I'm interested in your search for the mermaids. I'd like to help if I can. If nothing else, maybe I'll learn something from the knowledge you've gathered over the years." It wasn't a lie – Jolie *was* interested in what he'd learned. Much like human society, mermaids had their own territories and customs, and it would be fascinating to see how much of that had filtered through to humans over the years. Her education was spotty at best, handed down through Irma and the few classes she'd been required to attend in accordance with mermaid law.

They were the outliers of their society, choosing to live on land more than in the water, and that had come from the sheer amount of guilt Jolie's grandfather had felt about holding Irma back from her love. They'd been given a blessing to live where they wished, and because humans were endlessly fascinating, they'd chosen land.

"Jolie?" Ted said.

Jolie started, realizing she'd drifted away again. "I'm sorry, I was daydreaming. What did you say?"

"I was asking if I could buy you lunch to thank you for your help today."

He could buy her lunch every day for the rest of their lives as far as Jolie was concerned.

"Yes, thank you, that would be nice. Why don't we get you oil, then we can stop and see if Prince is around, and after that I'll take you to a cool little place on the water for food."

"Sounds great. And, Jolie – did you really mean that?"

"Mean what?"

"That you'd like to help me with my research? You have invaluable local knowledge. I can compensate you, as a research assistant, and then I won't feel so guilty taking up your time. I mean, if it's really of interest to you and not just politeness on your part."

"You're offering me a job?" Jolie's mouth dropped open. Nobody had ever offered her a job before. They'd never needed jobs, not really. The guesthouse was a delightful diversion, but their coffers were filled from the treasures found in the ocean over the years. Gold held a lot of value among humans, and selling a few pieces here and there was more than enough for the women to live on. Their needs were simple.

"Yes. Part-time, of course. Or just a few hours here and there, depending how much time you spend helping me out. I can offer reasonable compensation and a stipend for meals and such while we're out in the field."

"In the field?" Jolie squinted her eyes and looked out at the scraggly brush of the island.

"Well, not a literal field," Ted said with a laugh. "That's just a research term for when you're onsite instead of reading books or hunting through articles on the internet."

"It sounds so professional. And exotic! Do I get to wear canvas shorts and a hat like Crocodile Dundee? Or Indiana Jones? Will we dig things up? Oh! Can I tell Mirra I'm a scientist now?" Jolie was bubbling with questions.

Ted laughed again, crossing his arms over his chest and leaning back against the truck to study her.

"There might be a few steps you need to take before calling yourself a scientist. Maybe we can get away with citizen scientist. Or naturalist. But really this is more about mythology than science, so – a different type of research."

"I'm going to need a proper hat," Jolie decided.

"I see you're listening closely."

"I hear you. But I like to dress the part. I'll need to have an appropriate uniform for my first job."

"Your... first?" Ted straightened at that, staring down at her, and Jolie warmed again as she looked up at him. He easily stood several inches taller than her and she had to tilt her head. "You've never had a job?"

"Well, I have a job. We're innkeepers. But it's all we've ever done. I've never had to go apply elsewhere for a job."

"Ahh, so your second job."

"Well, my first *real* job, where somebody outside my family is hiring me. This is great. What kind of shoes will I need?"

"Shoes?" Ted looked down at her flip-flops and then scanned her legs. It was just a flick of his eyes, but Jolie caught it.

"Sure. Will we be hiking a lot?"

"I can't say. I may need to defer to you for instructions on where to hunt down more information."

"In that case, it'll be likely a mix of land and water. There's a lot to show you."

"I can't tell you how delighted I am to hear that." Ted quoted a number for compensation that made Jolie's eyebrows rise, and she readily agreed.

Imagine that! Earning her own money. It was something she'd never even considered; she'd never really wanted for anything she couldn't have. What was there to need? They had the ocean, they had food, and they had their health – a pretty dress or two and a few bangles to wear, and she was good. Most of the time she went barefoot, and Jolie rarely needed to take a purse anywhere on island. The idea of making her own money, separate from her family, was an intriguing one and filled her with a sense of pride.

"A research assistant," Jolie laughed, putting her hand out to shake Ted's. His warm palm engulfed hers and a zap of energy shot through their connected palms. Jolie held on when Ted jolted, her eyes meeting his, to see what he would do.

"That was odd. I didn't think it was dry enough here for static electricity," he said, pulling his hand away and rubbing it on his pants. He looked around the garage for anything that might have caused the electrical current he'd felt.

Jolie rolled her eyes behind his back, but only said, "Maybe we're just tapping into the energy of the island."

"Maybe," Ted muttered, and pulled out his recorder to murmur into it about his observation while he walked around the garage. She might as well have been invisible, Jolie realized.

"All finished?" Jolie asked when he finally turned back.

"Um, yes. Shall I follow you?"

"Yes." Please, Jolie thought as she walked away, *please* follow me – until the end of time.

CHAPTER 9

*T*ed breathed out a sigh of relief once he was in his own truck. He'd have to figure out how to be around Jolie in small doses, as she was one of the most distracting women he'd ever met. He wondered if she had any idea of her... potency. She had to, Ted thought, as he shifted into reverse and pulled the truck from the garage, waiting while Jolie keyed in the code to close the door. Women like her packed a punch *because* they were fully aware of their power.

Which was equal parts admirable and terrifying, as far as Ted was concerned.

He wished he'd been able to video her while she'd told the story of Nalachi and Irmine. It was as though she'd gone to another place – her face soft, her tone wistful – and he'd been so caught up in the story and her retelling of it that he hadn't even realized he'd grabbed her hand. How foolish of him. Ted shook his head. It was deeply unprofessional and it certainly crossed lines.

And now you've gone and asked her to work for you.

The little voice in his head that questioned everything he did was having a fit at his most recent burst of brilliance. Sure, it would put him and Jolie in close proximity most days, but as far as he was concerned, this was the only situation that would allow him to do so and not cross any lines. By hiring her as his assistant, Ted was neatly putting Jolie into a professional relationship with him. As a rule follower, he wouldn't be inclined to think about or treat her as anything other than a colleague. And that, in turn, would save him from having to see Irma's look of disappointment in him when she realized he had a crush on her daughter.

He definitely did not want to disappoint Irma. She struck him as the kind of woman who could make him feel ashamed of his thoughts or actions without ever having to deliver more than a soft warning. The idea of invoking her wrath was too much for Ted to imagine.

It would no longer be a problem, Ted reminded himself as he followed Jolie's truck to the main road. Jolie had gone from the gorgeous innkeeper to a colleague. It wouldn't do to think of the generous curve of her bosom, or the way her face came alive from within when she laughed. She was grace and elegance and a walking wet dream.

He'd been even more charmed by her when she'd snorted out a laugh – an indelicate sound coming from a goddess like her. The look of surprise and embarrassment on her face only strengthened her appeal, and Ted had kept his head under the hood of the truck longer than necessary when he'd checked the oil. He'd needed to calm his racing heart.

Get it out of your system, Macalister.

Flicking the radio on, Ted let the tuner scan until some bouncy reggae pumped out. Rolling down his window – manually – he let the island breezes in. This wasn't a bad way to conduct research, Ted thought. He was on a beautiful island with a research assistant who had an in with people in town – nope, there were certainly worse ways to work. He congratulated himself on doing what he'd come here to do: balance work and relaxation.

She looked like someone he'd once known.

Despite his promises to himself, Ted's thoughts were drawn back to Jolie. There was something about her that niggled at his brain, and it wasn't just the fact that she was drop-dead gorgeous. There was a familiarity there. The lines of her face, the movement of her body, the way she laughed. When she'd sung for him, it was as if someone had pulled back a curtain in his brain and he could see a movie playing out – the two tragic lovers on the beach. Except in the movie, it wasn't Irmine and Nalachi tangled together, waves washing over their hot skin as they rolled together on the beach. No, it had been Jolie and Ted, his mouth hot on hers, her body lush under his hands. It was no surprise he'd reached for her in that moment – the vision had been so vivid that Ted had been grateful he was wearing loose shorts and that Jolie had kept her gaze on the statue above them as she'd finished her story. Even now, a flush of embarrassment washed through him as he thought about his physical response to her.

Just a crush, Ted repeated to himself as he followed Jolie into a gravel parking lot in front of a mechanic's shop. Simple pheromones. There was no memory, he'd never met Jolie before, and the only future they had together was a professional one.

He'd do well to remember that, Ted lectured himself as her long and deliciously curvy legs extended from her truck.

Even if he had to do so every minute of the day.

CHAPTER 10

*J*olie had tamped down on her thoughts of winning over Ted for the time being as her excitement at being employed took over. It was just a silly part-time gig, Jolie told herself – but even so, she couldn't stop smiling. A job! Why hadn't she considered going out and getting a job before? She supposed it was because she was mainly satisfied with her life and hadn't needed anything else to fill any voids. But now?

It kind of felt like she was learning to be a strong independent woman who didn't need a man. Except she did need a man. Very much so. But that was her choice, wasn't it? Need as in wanted his hands on her, sure, but need as in couldn't live her life without him? Not likely. She'd done fine before Ted and she would be fine after him, if he chose to leave the island. And leave her.

Liar, her brain whispered, and Jolie shoved that particular thought aside. It wouldn't do any good to peer too far into the future at the moment. For now, she needed to let things play out as they would. Best not to toy with fate.

"Is this the restaurant?" Ted asked from behind her. She'd pulled to the side of the main road that ran the waterfront toward town, and had gotten out of her truck, waiting for Ted to do the same.

"Nope. I thought I might start you off with some introductions to locals who can offer more insight to the stories of sirens here." Jolie stopped and leaned over a cement wall that surrounded a little courtyard in front of a small boxy cottage. She imagined Prince could command quite a price for the property, being oceanfront and close to town, but she doubted he would ever sell his home. He would pass it down to family for generations to come.

The man himself sat in the shade of a tree, humming to himself as he tied lures for his fishing line.

"Prince, good day. How are you?" Jolie said, waving at him. With a shock of close-cropped white hair, deep brown skin, and a mile-wide smile, Prince was always a welcome sight.

"My goddess! You've come to visit a decrepit ol' man. I can't believe my own eyes," Prince said, motioning her to come in. "Bring de stranger in with you too."

"There's nothing decrepit about you, Prince. You spend longer hours on the water than anyone half your age." Jolie laughed and pressed a kiss to the old man's cheek.

"Naw, I can feel age creeping on. Deep in my bones." Prince shook his head sadly.

"Have you run out of the balm Mirra made for you?"

"I did."

"You know you only have to call us for more."

"Don't want to be no bother." Prince laughed, and rocked backward to eye Ted. "Now, where your manners at, girl? Who dis?"

"This is Dr. Theodore Macalister. He's staying with us at the Laughing Mermaid for the summer. He's here to study mermaids."

"Is he now? What kind of doctor? He gonna slice 'em up like I do my fish?" Prince peered around Jolie at Ted.

"Ah, no. That is most definitely not my plan. Please, call me Ted, by the way. Your name?"

"I'm Prince." The men shook hands and Jolie eased back, letting Ted take over the conversation.

"It's nice to meet you. I'm a literature professor. I'm more interested in the stories and myths of the mermaids than I am in catching one. Though I'd likely think I'd died and gone to heaven if I ever did see a mermaid."

"It's a sight dat stays with you, dat's for sure." Prince held his fist to his heart, his hands weathered with calluses. "Your heart isn't de same after."

"You've seen them?" Ted exclaimed, and immediately crouched so their eyes were on the same level. "I'd love to hear more if you don't mind sharing."

Prince studied Ted for a moment.

"Let me see your eyes."

Ted removed his sunglasses and met Prince's gaze. Prince held the look for a while before muttering to himself and nodding once.

"I tell you. But not today. I'm almost late for lunch with Maria. You know how she gets." Prince slanted a look at Jolie.

"Do not cross that woman, and do not show up late for lunch."

"'Dat's the truth. But I'll stay a moment. Jolie, can you get de shell for de doctor? I think he needs to hold it, den we see what we dealin' with here."

"What shell?" Ted looked to Jolie, his eyes a tawny green in the sunlight.

Her heart did a little flip in her chest. "Prince has a real mermaid artifact. It's one of his most prized possessions."

"Is that so? I'd be honored to see it," Ted said, his words holding not even a trace of skepticism.

Jolie admired his willingness to ask questions and learn, withholding all judgement, and wondered if she would be capable of doing the same if their positions were switched. She ducked into Prince's cottage, knowing he kept his prize shell in a bowl by the door, and then returned to the garden where Ted now sat on a small bench in the shade next to Prince.

"Here you are," Jolie said. She handed it to Prince first, knowing his attachment to it – not to mention the fact that the man liked to showboat a little.

"Now dis here? A real mermaid shell. Plucked from de ocean when we were diving for conch – back in de days when dat was allowed and all." Prince winked at Jolie. The island had recently added new rules to the marine park, one of which was to create a more sustainable means of fishing for conch. It was nice to see the island was taking ocean conservation seriously, and Jolie was happy to see the reefs already thriving. "Now dis shell called to me, you hear? It pulled me like a magnet to it. Just lying dere in de sand, nothing around it. All but called my name. It's magick, I tell you. True and true."

"Is that so?"

"It is. Tell me what you feel when you hold it." Prince handed the shell to Ted.

Jolie held her breath as he turned it over in his hands, examining the soft sheen and colors. A flush of pink covered his cheeks and those gorgeous eyes of his pinned her where she stood.

He saw them. Jolie was as sure of it as she was of her next breath. The world around them seemed to drop away as she shared in his vision – limbs tangled, mouths locked, damp skin pressed together… It was enough to make her take a deep breath and close her eyes. When she opened them again, he'd looked away to a beaming Prince.

"Ah… hmm," Ted said, carefully considering his words.

"No need to tell me." Prince held up a hand, laughing softly. "I see de passion on your face."

"What do you see when you hold it?" Ted asked, quickly diverting the conversation though the pink still clung to his cheeks. Jolie found it charming, this small tell of his, and hoped she'd still be able to see his blush once he got a tan.

"For me? Simple pleasures. Lying in a hammock. Ocean breezes."

"Is there a rule about what it's meant to show? Why is it different for different people?"

"No rules, not dat I know of. Just everyone has a different response. You take your own meaning from it. Now," Prince said. He stood and pulled a sleek iPhone from his pocket, surprising Ted. "I be late for lunch and Maria gonna give me an earful. You'll come back." It wasn't a question, but an order.

"Of course. Should I make an appointment?" Ted asked.

Prince's shoulders bounced as he laughed. "No appointments here, man. You just pass by. If I'm home, I'm home."

"Wonderful. Thank you for your time. Maybe next time, if you don't mind, I can record you? I'd love to hear your stories about seeing the mermaids."

"Time enough for dat. I'll see you," Prince said. After making sure his shell was back in the right spot, he ambled down the street, leaning on a beautifully carved driftwood walking stick.

"Doesn't he need to lock up?" Ted asked, worry etching his face as he slid his sunglasses back on.

"Nobody here would dare mess with Prince's stuff. That would be like stealing from your grandfather."

"He's nice."

"He is. And he'll enjoy nothing more than telling you all his mermaid stories. He has some good ones. Bring a cooler of beer and you'll be chatting all day."

"Duly noted. Have you heard his stories?"

"Most of them," Jolie said, following him from the courtyard and latching the small gate behind her.

"I can go without you then. I don't want to take up all your time."

"We'll see what I have on my schedule the day you decide to go. Lunch?" Jolie asked.

"Yes, please. I'm famished."

"This way then. We can walk." Jolie indicated a thatched hut just down the road. Smoke poured from a grill set up in the back and a line snaked around the corner.

"It looks busy," Ted said.

Jolie wondered if he was going to ask her about the shell or just file it away for his notes. There was no way he couldn't have felt something – she saw what he'd seen.

"It's a popular local spot. Mixed grill. Eat by the water-front. Keep it easy and hear the local gossip."

"Perfect. That's about as far away from my polished Bostonian lunch restaurants as I can get."

"Fancy guy, are you?" Jolie asked as she waved hello to people before joining the line.

"Not fancy, typically. If I'm on my own I usually work through lunch or grab a sandwich from the cafeteria. But if I'm going out to lunch it's because I got roped into a meeting with colleagues or we have to entertain donors – that kind of thing."

"It sounds... fussy," Jolie decided, turning to look out at the sun shimmering over the turquoise water. "And let me guess – bland food?"

"Depends where we eat. But yes, a bit bland, I suppose."

"This may look humble, but it's got a kick. You'll enjoy it," Jolie said.

"I imagine I will. The scent alone is enough to pull anyone in."

"You're very easygoing." Jolie looked up at him. "I haven't seen you break a sweat yet."

"I most definitely am sweating. It's summer in the tropics."

"But you just kind of go along for the ride. Nothing seems to faze you. Even the shell."

"Ah. Well, I wouldn't say the shell left me unaffected." Ted cleared his throat, then was interrupted by a woman leaning over the counter of the shack.

"Mixed grill?" she asked.

"Sure – two please. Oh, and" – Ted craned his neck to look over the counter – "two iced teas."

Jolie would have preferred an ice-cold beer, but she suspected Ted would never drink on the job. She wondered what it would take to ruffle his feathers or make him break his rules. It would be an interesting challenge, she thought with a smile.

"What's that smile for?" Ted had frozen in place, looking down at her with a can of iced tea in each hand.

"What? Oh, nothing."

"That's good. It looked predatory. I don't envy anyone on the other side of it."

"Really? Why predatory?"

"Because you looked like a cat about to go on a hunt. Or like you would eat someone alive. Here, drink this instead," Ted said. He dropped the cans on a small table-top, then hurried to pick up their baskets of food.

Predatory! Jolie huffed. She had only been thinking about how to… okay, yeah, maybe he was right. Damn, the man had good intuition.

CHAPTER 11

"*T*ell me about the oracle," Ted said as he dug into his food with enthusiasm.

Jolie blinked at him, her mind trying to keep up with his quicksilver conversational pivots. "The... oh. The mermaid oracle?"

"Right. That one. I've never heard that mentioned in my studies, so I find it interesting how you said it so naturally. It seemed like something you were fairly confident about. Can you elaborate on what you know of this oracle? Is there just one? How does a mermaid become an oracle? What kind of things do they prophesize about? Can they make rules and laws? *Are* there rules and laws in mermaid society?"

Jolie paused and took a sip of her iced tea, not saying anything.

Ted looked up and ducked his head, a sheepish smile on his face. "Sorry, too many questions. Let's start with the first." Ted pushed his little recorder between them. "What can you tell me about the oracle?"

Jolie thought for a moment about how she wanted to approach this. It would probably be best if she had a conversation with Irma and Mirra about what to reveal about the mermaids. But on the flip side, the oracle had said Ted was the one for her. There was no way he could be her destiny if the secrets of mermaid society were kept from him.

Jolie leaned forward – she would tell him about the oracle, but then nothing more until she spoke with the others.

"I think she serves many purposes, much like an oracle in any society," Jolie began, then stopped when Ted held up a finger.

"She?"

"Yes, she. It's always a she."

"Hmm, a matriarchal oracle. Interesting."

"We –" Jolie stopped herself, realizing she had been about to say, 'We do value powerful women.' Instead she said, "We at the Laughing Mermaid strongly believe in a matriarchal lineage. We like powerful women. So, for me, I think it's cool that the oracle would be female."

"Makes sense – and I agree. Women are powerful beyond belief."

"It's nice of you to acknowledge that," Jolie teased. Then she continued, "The oracle plays many roles. She can be called upon to look to the future, say in times of uncertainty or war. But each of the merpeople receive a reading on his or her sixteenth birthday."

"And what is the nature or purpose of that reading?"

"Have you read Harry Potter?" Jolie asked.

A small smile hovered on Ted's lips. "Naturally."

"In some respects, the oracle can be like the Sorting Hat. She might identify someone who is destined to rule, or someone who will be a great healer – things like that."

"Fascinating. So, her readings are what places people into their jobs?" Ted paused and raised a finger as he thought. "I guess I never thought about mermaids having jobs. That's odd as well. But every society has some sort of jobs – from food collection to minding the children. I suppose it would be no different for mermaids."

"Exactly. But not always jobs. Sometimes it's to reveal a purpose. Perhaps a mermaid is meant to meet someone." Jolie paused, not meeting Ted's eyes, and then hurried on. "Or perhaps they're intended to play a pivotal role in guiding the direction of their society. It's not really a set-in-stone kind of reading. The oracle says what she sees, and each mermaid must determine what it means to them."

"Are the fortunes revealed?"

"Not always, but yes, it would be common enough to return and tell your family about your reading." But Jolie hadn't shared hers.

"There would be no pushback if a fortune isn't shared?"

"Maybe some. But you have to understand that mermaids are very accepting of individuality. The society as a whole supports each other and trusts that each member will make the right decision for themselves, while also not bringing harm to the society."

"That sounds very trusting. Almost too trusting. But perhaps I'm cynical." Ted shrugged.

"Not all societies put the greater good over individual choice. But because mermaids are a small and secretive society, they must weigh the benefit to the whole while also ensuring each member feels confident making choices that best suit themself."

"That sounds tricky."

"It can be at times, I'm sure. But I think mermaids ultimately value the greater good of their entire society over one individual's wish. The other thing they'll often do is work with a mermaid to help them toward the fulfillment of their individual destiny. It makes it far less likely for a mermaid to go off on their own, and keeps the collective good at the forefront of their mind."

"That's interesting. So, say a mermaid had a reading that said they were destined to be a great leader – the others would help them to achieve it?"

"Yes – they trust their oracle." Jolie took a sip of her iced tea. She'd almost said 'we' again. She'd have to be careful with these discussions.

"And for those who don't reveal their reading?"

"There's an understanding that it's a private matter, likely of the heart, and in time all will be revealed."

"It sounds like mermaids are a patient bunch."

"They can be. I don't think it would be wise to anger them, though."

"Do not anger mermaids." Ted made a show of pretending to write down the instruction, and Jolie found herself laughing out loud again.

"You're pretty funny for a stuffy college professor."

"Well, I can't say that humor's my strong suit, but I have my moments."

"I get that. My humor often misses the mark." Jolie

sighed and pushed the rest of her food away. "Apparently I can sting a little too hard."

"I highly doubt that. You've been nothing but nice since I arrived."

"Oh, I have a bit of a nasty streak in me, Doctor. Don't be fooled." Jolie smiled, softening her words.

"We all do. That's human nature."

"Right." Jolie toasted him with her can and wondered what he'd do when he found out she wasn't actually human.

CHAPTER 12

*J*olie left Ted at the supermarket with detailed instructions on how to get back to the guest-house, and left for home. On impulse, she swung by Lola's shop to see if she had anything new for Jolie to peruse. Even though she didn't typically spend a lot of money, Jolie had one weakness – jewelry. She couldn't help herself; she loved layering all sorts of beads and bangles, enjoying the shimmer and shine of adorning herself in sparkly things.

Lola had settled nicely into the rhythm of island life, particularly now that she connected with Siren Island in such a different way than most. Her shop was thriving, she was happy and in love, and she and Jolie had developed a deep bond. Jolie loved Mirra, of course, but it was nice to have someone other than her sister to talk to.

Lola's shop was set up right on the water, in one of the island's original cottages. She'd overhauled it, adding her own personal touch, and turned the back garden into a hang-out spot where artists could paint the day away with a cup of coffee. One night a week, Lola hosted a paint-and-wine night, and it had become wildly successful. The little spot had sat empty for years until she'd breathed life into it, and now locals and tourists alike could often be found chatting at the shop, having a drink, or selling their own artworks. Lola was very supportive of local island art, and her shop boasted many a talented artist.

"Hey lady," Jolie called, stepping into the cool interior of the shop. Large bamboo-style fans swooped lazily above her head, and the shutters on the windows were thrown open to encourage the ocean breezes. Lola, her hair piled on her head and a neon pink sarong wound around her body, looked up from the notes she was making on a pad by the cash register.

"Jolie! I haven't seen you in a while. How are you?" Lola crossed the room to hug Jolie; then she pulled back, her hands on her arms, and studied Jolie's face. "Hmm, I think you need tea."

"I just had a tea."

"Well, have another."

"Fine," Jolie grumbled, annoyance lancing through her. That in itself was such an unusual feeling for Jolie that she paused and took a deep breath.

"Check out my newest shipment while I brew you a cup. This artist is from Brazil." Lola gestured to the counter where various woven pouches sat. Each pouch, small enough to contain a necklace or earrings, was designed with intricate patterns.

"Pretty," Jolie remarked.

Lola chuckled. "No, silly. Those are just the jewelry bags. Look inside them." Jolie opened the first bag and pulled out a necklace – hammered gold links with shimmering amethyst and citrine stones.

"Ohhhhh," Jolie breathed.

"See? I thought you'd like those. The pieces are more exotic than most, but use a lot of lovely crystals and stones without looking too…" Lola held up a finger and twirled it by her head.

"Like you're in a hippie commune and about to run naked through the woods?"

"Something like that. Though that actually sounds quite nice. I'd say they're more elevated crystal pieces." Lola brought over two cups of mint tea and placed them on the counter.

"I'd like this one," Jolie said, holding up a necklace layered in alternating silver and gold chains, with the tiniest of moonstone and rose quartz beads. It shimmered in the light, and Jolie could feel the gentle pulse of love radiating from the stones.

"Looking for love, are we?" Lola said, narrowing her eyes at Jolie as she went to wrap the necklace. Jolie pulled the necklace back, and fixed it around her neck, feeling the stones warm against her chest.

"I've found it. But he doesn't know it yet," Jolie blurted out.

Lola froze. "No way! You can't tell me the great Jolie has fallen. I thought you never wanted to be with one person?" Lola winced as she realized how that might sound, and held up a hand in apology. "Sorry, I wasn't calling you a ho. You know I'm all for freedom in choosing your lovers."

"I know you weren't. And you're right – I haven't been

particularly focused on settling down because I've always been waiting for him."

"Him who? And how did you know?" Lola glanced at the delicate watch on her wrist and then at the minibar behind the desk. "Is it too early for alcohol?"

"We live on an island. It's never too early for alcohol. I saw a woman leaving the bar with a to-go beer first thing this morning."

"I imagine her day was the better for it." Lola chuckled and pulled out a bottle of tequila. "We're just going to sip a little with our mint tea."

"Fine by me," Jolie said. Alcohol didn't affect her the way it did most humans, so she could drink and feel pleasant but never truly lose her head.

"Now. Tell me first how you've always been searching for this man. And why you never told me."

"I never told anyone," Jolie admitted, pulling out a stool that was tucked on the other side of the counter and plopping down into it. She watched as Lola shook the tequila over some ice and added a twist of lime before pouring a small amount into two translucent blue glasses. "Not even Mirra."

"Oh, she's going to kill you for telling me first," Lola breathed.

"She's not going to know I told you first." Jolie shot Lola a dark look, and Lola laughed, holding up her hand.

"Down, girl."

"I've just always seen this one person for me. I was…" Jolie hesitated, then decided against telling Lola about the oracle. She wasn't sure about the rules there – whether Lola would have gotten a reading at some point, or if she'd missed out because it took so long for her to discover her roots – but that was something to ponder for another day. "I had a dream, a recurring dream, and this man has always been in it. I've always known."

"What's the dream like?"

"Laughter. A lot of laughter. Babies. Love. Hot sex." Jolie sighed.

"Sounds like a great dream."

"It is a great dream. And I think I love the laughter part the most."

"Of course. I can see that."

"I've always looked. I've been convinced I could find this man. And yet, for years, nothing."

"Until…?"

"Until he showed up on our doorstep as our newest guest."

"Ohhhhhhh…" Lola took half her tequila in one gulp.

"Exactly."

"I want the full details," Lola demanded, then listened while Jolie told her everything she'd learned about one Dr. Theodore Macalister.

"And I snorted," Jolie said, slapping her hand on the counter before taking her own sip of the tequila. "I do *not* snort."

"Like a laughing-so-hard snort?"

"Yes."

"You said you wanted laughter," Lola pointed out, and smiled when Jolie glared at her. "What? It's nice to see you out of sorts. You're always so wildly confident. I like this side of you."

"I don't."

"Well, of course not. You're vulnerable – something that's not in character for you. But that's a good thing."

"What am I supposed to do? He doesn't even see me."

"Oh, he sees you. No man alive could miss you, Jolie." Lola laughed again and began categorizing the necklaces in front of her as she talked. "But it also sounds like he's very focused and prefers to follow the rules. It would be improper for him to make a move on you as a guest at your resort, and – well, now you work for him, too."

"Oh shit." Jolie realized what she'd done. "I just put myself firmly in the do-not-touch category."

"Correct. But it sounds like you're excited about the job?"

"I am! I've never had a job before. And it sounds so fancy – research assistant. I could put it on one of those…" Jolie waved her hand around.

"Résumés?" Lola laughed.

"Yes, those things."

"I highly doubt you'll ever need one."

"But I could make one if I wanted."

"That you could." Lola leaned forward and squeezed Jolie's hand. "What do you want, Jolie?"

"I want him to see me. And to fall for me – all of me. Not me using magick or siren wiles on him, but just *me*."

"Then you have to give it time. He's here for a while. Don't push this. You have a habit of bulldozing through things to get what you want. It's served you in the past, but I suspect that if you do it in this instance, you're going to scare him away."

"I am used to getting what I want," Jolie admitted, and

took a sip of her honey-sweetened mint tea. "And yes, I know how shitty that sounds."

"It does sound shitty. But I know you, and I know it's not you being a jerk. It's just that most people are unable to match the force of who you are as a person. And I will say this – I would never, *ever*, ask you to shade your light to make it more comfortable for others. Jolie, you are a force. A powerful one. And that's perfectly fine. However, when dealing with a man like Ted, you might want to be patient."

"Not my strong suit."

"You'll learn," Lola laughed as Jolie glowered into her drink. "It's nice to see you have faults like the rest of us."

"Bite me."

CHAPTER 13

*W*hat a curious thing it was to be out of one's comfort zone, Jolie mused on the drive home. As Lola had not-so-gently pointed out, most people experienced this feeling regularly. Rarely did people sail through life feeling confident in everything they did. Jolie was learning that she was an anomaly, in more ways than one, and the feeling was a bit humbling. If anything, it was opening her worldview to the fact that not everything came as easily for others as it did for her.

Which meant she'd have to adjust her expectations of Ted.

Jolie allowed herself to daydream on the drive home, knowing she'd have to push some of these thoughts away to focus on being patient with Ted and hoping he'd come around to liking her. But, for now, she let her mind play over the oracle's vision for her and how that melded with the man she'd met in real life.

If anything, he was better than she'd imagined. Sure, she'd likely find he had some flaws – what man didn't?

But Jolie hadn't expected him to have a quicksilver mind and a dry wit. It added a level of appeal that had been lacking in many of her past lovers, and she wondered if she had a thing for brainy types that she'd never tapped into before.

It made her want to impress him.

Wasn't that just something? Not impress him with her body or her beauty – she wanted to make him laugh, or find interesting things for him to research. Taking Lola's advice to be patient, Jolie began to catalog all the various mermaid things she could teach Ted about.

Still mulling it over, she pulled to a stop at the Laughing Mermaid and got out of the truck. Noticing that Ted had made it back already, Jolie beelined for the kitchen, hoping to have a chat with Irma and Mirra.

Irma was typing on her laptop at the kitchen table. "You've been gone a while," she commented.

"I'm sorry. Did you need the truck? You could have called me."

"No bother. I went to the shops yesterday." Irma waved it away and returned to her typing. Jolie opened the fridge and found a half-full bottle of rosé. Pouring herself a glass, she settled across from Irma and let out a sigh. When her mother continued to type, Jolie sighed more loudly.

Mirra breezed into the kitchen, pointed at Jolie, and asked, "What's this one moping about?"

"She's been pouting here for a few minutes, but I haven't gotten to her yet. I need to finish this response to a guest inquiry."

"I am not pouting." Jolie pushed out her lip.

"That's a pout if I've ever seen one," Mirra laughed. "What's got you in a funk? That's not usual for you."

"I need to talk to you both. About something serious, actually," Jolie said. When Irma's hand stilled on the keyboard, she added, "Go on, finish your email, Mother."

"Just one moment."

Mirra quietly pulled out two glasses and poured the last of the wine. She brought the glasses to the table, sliding one to her mother and keeping the other for herself.

Once Irma had finished typing, she closed her laptop and she and Mirra both looked at Jolie expectantly.

"Here's the thing: I need to know how much I can tell Ted about us."

"Us as in *us,* or us as in mermaids?" Irma asked, taking a sip of her wine.

"Both, I guess," Jolie said, wiping a drop of condensation from the side of her glass with one finger. "I feel like I want to just tell him everything and then I remember who he is and I'm worried just how much he'll put in his paper and then it all gets muddled."

"Why do you want to tell him everything? That's not like you at all." Mirra frowned at her across the table, worry settling onto her pretty features. Today her blond hair hung in a loose braid over her shoulders and she wore a simple white cotton slip dress.

"She's right. You're one of the first to advocate for protecting our secrets. What makes you want to tell Ted? Is it because he's a believer? Or that he's researched mermaids?"

Because he's mine, Jolie almost blurted out. She closed her mouth, looking from her mother to her sister.

"Ah," Irma said, reaching over to squeeze Jolie's hand. "I see."

"He's your person." Mirra nodded, happiness flooding her face. "That's amazing, Jolie. You've been searching for so long."

"What? I didn't say that. And how did you know I've been searching? I've enjoyed my time with men, is all."

"You've been searching. I know you well enough to know that if you hadn't been, you would have settled down with that ship's captain who came through a few years back. What was his name? Edward?"

"Ah." Jolie held her hand to her heart and they all took a brief moment to salute Edward and his handsome crew. Jolie was absolutely sure she hadn't been the only one to sample the goods there.

"He would have been an adventurous life partner," Irma agreed. "But again, not for you. This one, however, seems to be."

"Why do you say that?" Jolie pushed her lip out, feeling a bit petulant about having to be vulnerable to them.

"Because you've never asked how much you can reveal to anyone before. Ever."

"Ugh. Fine. He's the one. The oracle showed me," Jolie said, taking a sip of her wine and peeking over the rim of her glass to see their reactions. Mirra gasped, and Irma simply smiled. She'd known, Jolie realized, though she wasn't sure how.

"You never would tell me your reading," Mirra said. "Will you now?"

Jolie recounted the reading, keeping an eye on Irma

the whole time. Then, while Mirra processed the information, she turned to Irma. "Why are you not surprised by this?"

"I knew he was the one for you when he walked off the plane. You aren't the only one who has been shown things, my love."

"Why didn't you tell me?" Jolie demanded.

"What, and miss this? Never. It's an absolute joy to see you flustered for once in your life, Jolie. This will be a great learning experience for you."

"A learning experience?" Jolie's voice went up an octave. "You look at my destiny as a *learning experience*?"

"Of course. If you aren't learning, you aren't living. Who wants to remain stagnant forever?"

"I find you very annoying right now," Jolie said, turning to glower into her wine.

"The tried and true test of time with mothers and daughters," Irma said, and laughed when Jolie slid her a dark look. "I'm going to get some food started."

"Jolie, do you really think this is him? The man you've been waiting for?" Mirra asked, her voice soft as she looked at her sister with worried eyes.

"I do. And who would have thought I had a thing for the brainy type?"

Irma laughed from where she stood at the counter, slicing up peppers for dinner, her hair tumbling over her shoulders and bracelets jingling at her wrists. She'd switched on a little speaker and reggae music pumped lightly into the room.

"He's not just brains. It's not like he's hard on the eyes, Jolie. And he's very fit. I like this pick for you. Smart, kind, and good-looking. And! He loves mermaids. This is all good stuff here," Mirra insisted.

"Is it? Because I've felt off-kilter since the moment I met him. And now I've gone and accepted a job from him."

"A job!" Mirra and Irma said in unison.

"Jinx," Jolie mumbled, draining her wine and getting up to go back to the fridge for more.

"Are you quitting the Laughing Mermaid? You know, in the business world they expect at least two weeks' notice." Irma put the peppers in a bowl and started on the onions.

"I'm not quitting working here. It's just a part-time job. I'll be a research assistant."

"Oh, how fancy! What will you wear? We need to try on some outfits. Do you think you'd look good in glasses? Like those heavy-framed black ones? Then you tie your hair up all tight and wear your glasses, and when you seduce him you toss the glasses across the room and let your hair tumble down…" Mirra trailed off and glanced guiltily over her shoulder at Irma.

"I suspect he would like that very much," Irma said, and Jolie groaned, burying her nose in her glass of wine at this fresh humiliation.

"I can't seduce him if I'm working for him. He barely notices me as it is. And he's exactly the type who would be put off by crossing any boundaries. If I didn't know better, I'd say he did this on purpose just so I wouldn't make a move on him."

"Why don't you ask him?" Irma asked, adding her onions to the bowl, then pulling out a large skillet.

"Ask him? Are you crazy? You want me to just ask if he hired me so I wouldn't make a move on him?"

"Ask him if he's attracted to you and would be interested in a date."

"You want *me* to ask *him* out?" Jolie pointed at her chest.

"It's not uncommon in this day and age," Mirra observed.

"I have *never* asked a man out before," Jolie said, outrage racing through her. "That's… well, that's just ridiculous."

"It's really not. Women do it all the time, you know. Plus, I think men probably find it helpful. It can be tricky to read the signs to know if someone is interested. I'm sure many are quite relieved to know when someone is interested in them. Men and women, I guess. I mean, it's pleasant to be asked out, isn't it? Probably even more so if the person isn't used to it…" Mirra trailed off again as she caught Jolie's look. "Sorry. Got it. Not asking him out."

"What does a research assistant do exactly, Jolie?"

"I think he primarily wants to compensate me for my time in helping him dig up more mermaid myths and legends, introducing him to other people on the island with stories, that kind of thing. I also get the feeling he's probably hiring me so he doesn't feel bad about taking up my time. He could have kept going all day today with just the few tidbits I've already told him."

"Jolie, you know there are no rules or curtain of silence about what you can say or not say about us. I've always left that to your discretion." Irma stirred the peppers and onions now frying in the skillet.

"But it feels like it's smart not to say anything."

"Why?" Mirra asked.

"Because. We should protect our people."

"And you think he'll bring harm to us?"

"He could. He has the clout to do it. He teaches at a freaking Ivy League school. People will actually listen to what he has to say. What if he reveals too much?"

"And what, Jolie?" Irma said, turning the heat down and looking over her shoulder at the table. "What do you think will happen?"

"They'll come after us!"

"You think we'd be killed? Captured? Kept like freaks behind bars to look at?"

Jolie shrugged. "Maybe."

"And you think your destiny – your match – is the type of person that would do something like this?"

"Maybe not him, but someone he speaks to might."

"Jolie." Irma moved around the counter to come stand by the table. She leaned down, putting her hands on the wood so her face was level with Jolie's. "Listen to me very carefully. What we accept and take for our normal is not what others will. If you think Dr. Macalister is going to bounce his way back to Boston, announce that mermaids are real, and a team of scientists will not only believe him but come to Siren Island and hunt us down, then you are more naïve than I thought."

"Hey!" Jolie glared at her.

"Well? Think about it. What's more likely is that he'll be laughed at or given a pat on the back while someone makes a crazy sign behind his head. They'll think he's gone off his rocker. One of the biggest reasons we've been able to stay hidden for all these years is simply that people refuse to believe in something outside their norm. It takes a lot of courage to believe in something you don't fully understand. I suspect most will brush aside anything he has to say under the assumption that he's just gotten too much sun."

"You think I'm overthinking this?"

"I think you will know the right thing to do when the time comes. Be patient, Jolie. See how this unfolds. Get to know him. Listen to your gut. Listen to your instincts. And then, trust your heart. You'll know if you want to share your story with him or not. There's no reason to rush into it all on the first day."

"She does have a tendency to rush…" Mirra trailed off again at Jolie's glare and gulped her wine.

"I'm not good at being patient." Jolie shot another look at Mirra, who stifled a giggle.

"Then you'll have to learn."

CHAPTER 14

"So, Ms. Research Assistant, what's the plan for today?" Mirra propped herself up on Jolie's bed and watched her sister get ready.

"I think the plan is to track down Prince and hear more of his stories."

"He's a good start. He's had plenty of encounters and certainly loves to spin a tale." Mirra nodded when Jolie held up a pair of breezy shorts with palm leaves splashed over them and a hot pink halter-style tank top.

"Not too bright?"

"No, it's fun. You live on an island. Go bright. And if you do any off-road wandering, shorts are a good choice."

"Okay." Jolie disappeared into the bathroom and Mirra's voice followed her there.

"Did you see Ted last night?"

"I did not. After our delightful conversation, I hid in my room like any normal wounded animal would."

"Oh, hush. You don't need to feel wounded just

because you're feeling vulnerable right now. Don't confuse the two."

"All I hear is, 'Be patient. Trust. Be uncomfortable.'" Jolie leaned out the door of her bathroom and looked at Mirra. "And frankly? It's annoying. I don't want to be patient. I've *been* patient. I've been waiting years for him. I want to jump him and show him why he should love me."

"But that's the easy part for you, Jo," Mirra said.

Jolie ducked her head back in the bathroom to study her face in the mirror. No blemishes, though dark circles ringed her eyes from poor sleep. "I think you're calling me a slut."

"I'm not calling you a slut," Mirra laughed. "Though you are definitely being a little bitchy this morning."

"Not redeeming yourself here," Jolie said as she finished up in the bathroom.

"Listen, you can sleep with a different guy every night of the week and I would not judge you. You have one life to live and you have every right to enjoy yourself. But what I'm saying is that going to bed with a man has never been an issue with you. You're confident and you enjoy a healthy round of sex with a man of your choosing. But don't confuse sex and intimacy."

"I'd say it's fairly intimate, Mirra. The man's pretty much all up in there." Jolie rolled her eyes as she packed a little leather backpack for the day.

"Fine. Intimate with your body, yes. But not your feelings. You always keep a wall up. You always *have* kept a wall up. Now that you see someone you really, really want

– well, the wall is crumbling and it's scary for you. You're in unchartered waters here."

"Got it. Rebuild my wall." Jolie nodded and slung the straps of the bag over her shoulders.

"No, you idiot. Be vulnerable. Learn about yourself in this new way. Open to him. Take this slow and see what kind of connection you can build with him. One that doesn't require him to drop his pants."

"What's the fun in that?"

"I suspect sex is a lot more fun with someone you love." Mirra rolled from the bed and stood, coming over to put her arms around Jolie.

"You wouldn't know."

"And neither would you. So, here's your chance to know. Don't rush this one, Jolie. Let it unfold. Savor it like you're unwrapping an extra special present, or sampling a fine dessert."

"I always rip the wrapping paper off my presents."

"Well, try something new this time."

"Fine." Jolie stuck her lip out and stamped her foot, pretending to have a tantrum.

"You could try holding your breath until you get your way."

"Maybe I'll just sit on him until he has to see me."

"By the looks of his muscles, I bet he could lift you right off. Have fun today!" Mirra called as she left Jolie's room and went back to her own. Jolie closed her door and went out into the morning sun to practice her patience.

Ted straightened from where he leaned against a palm tree, a thermos in hand, and smiled at her. A button-down khaki shirt with the sleeves rolled to his elbows, khaki shorts, and worn hiking boots completed his "island explorer" look – at least that was what Jolie was calling it – and he looked prepared for anything. Her stomach did a funny little shiver just looking at him, and she wanted nothing more than to drag the man back to her bedroom and see if she could make him sweat.

"Good morning," Jolie said. "Did you sleep well?"

"I did, thank you. I enjoyed a light dinner on my terrace and wrote up notes from what we saw yesterday. And you?"

"Not as well as I would've liked. But the sun is shining and we're off on an adventure, so that's all good." Jolie shot him a smile when he opened the door of the truck for her.

"Is it an adventure for you? I wondered if showing guests around the island was exciting or if it had grown boring."

"No, it's fun. Plus, it's my first day on my new job and I'm also excited about that." Jolie glanced down at her outfit. "I hope I am appropriately attired for work, sir."

"You look fine," Ted said as he shifted the truck into gear.

"Gee, thanks," Jolie said, shooting him a look.

"Sorry – I mean you look perfectly appropriate for your job as a research assistant."

It wasn't exactly the praise she had been looking for, but Jolie suspected Ted had years of practice in not overstepping boundaries with his students. She really needed to stop fishing for compliments and focus on her work. Her *work*, she reminded herself, with her new *boss*.

"Thank you. I want to make sure I do everything right."

"It's okay if you don't. First, I haven't even given you a job description, so it's not like you can screw up too much there. Secondly, even if you do make mistakes, it's no big deal. That's how people learn."

"I bet you're a good teacher, aren't you?"

"Well, that's hard to say." Ted laughed and ran his hand over his chin as he thought about it. "I really enjoy teaching. More than I actually ever thought I would. It's pushed me outside of my comfort zone and forced me to talk to people – and in large lecture halls at that. I hope my passion for the subject matter shines through and that at least some of my students come away having learned something new."

Jolie pictured Ted in front of a lecture hall, maybe with a suit coat on, his eyes alight with excitement as he discussed centuries-old myths and legends. She imagined more than one student had a crush on him, as the image alone made her sigh. Hot for teacher, indeed.

"Based on what I've already learned about you, I bet your class is fairly popular."

"Well, there is a bit of a waiting list to get in."

"That doesn't surprise me in the least. I think when you're enthusiastic about your subject matter, most people will enjoy listening to you speak. What would you do if you didn't teach or didn't have to worry about money?"

Ted cleared his throat uncomfortably, and Jolie looked at him with interest.

"I'm guessing this means you *don't* have to worry about money?"

"Well, no, not really. A smart investment when I was young."

"That's fantastic. Good for you! You could have sat on your butt and done nothing, and instead you followed your passion. Not everyone would do that, you know."

"I wonder how happy people would be if they could simply follow their passions. The world would be a better place."

"If money wasn't the driver? Sure, I can see that. Though they say to follow your passion and the money will follow."

"Hard to do if you have mouths to feed at home."

"That's true – the choice is harder if you have children to care for. Have you ever thought of that?"

"What, how hard it is to feed a family while pursuing your passion?"

"No, silly. Having kids. Or do you already have some?"

"No." A smile slid across Ted's face. "There are none of my progeny walking around. But I really like kids. I teach college-age, but I think I'd like to be a father one day."

Jolie's ovaries perked up at that and she shifted, turning to look out at the turquoise water. They followed the road toward town, and Jolie wondered if he would be happy here on the island. Raising kids here, leaving his job in Boston – would it be something he would entertain? The island didn't have much in the way of university-level courses; maybe he could help with that.

"What about you?"

"Oh, me?" Jolie glanced back at him. "Yes, I've always wanted to be a mother."

"Really?"

"Is that surprising to you? Don't I look motherly?"

"I don't know that it's possible for anyone to 'look' motherly. Mothers come in all shapes and sizes. I'm just surprised because you strike me as very confident and independent. And more and more women these days are choosing not to have children."

"I don't think being confident or independent precludes you from having children."

"The confident part, no. But the independent part, yes. I mean, the very definition of a child – in government terms, at least – is 'dependent.'"

"Sure, in the physical sense. But I don't think you have to lose who you are as a person to be a mother."

"Ah, you're talking about the existential independence. No, I don't think you lose who you are when you become a parent. Rather, I think you find another dimension of yourself. Perhaps we can call it an expansion of you."

"And, for a woman, quite literally." Jolie mimicked holding a large baby belly in front of her and Ted laughed.

"Well, Miss Jolie, I hope you get your babies someday, then, and never lose your spirit or your wit."

"Thank you," Jolie said, biting her lip and turning to look out the window again. It was a reminder that he looked at her only in the business sense. She shouldn't feel disheartened by his words; the man just didn't know yet what was sitting right in front of him. Mirra was right. All she needed was just a little patience. As if she'd conjured it, the radio switched to Guns n' Roses and the song "Patience" came on.

Funny, universe, Jolie thought as she glared out the window, real funny.

CHAPTER 15

*P*rince was having a coffee in his garden when they pulled up, his gaze out to the water. A wide grin stretched his face, the two missing front teeth only adding to his charm, and he lifted a hand in hello.

"Back so soon, eh? De mermaid shell will call to its own."

"Is that so? I'd love to look at it again. And I've brought a few things of my own to share," Ted said, smiling at Prince over the wall to his garden. "Do you have time for a chat?"

"I have all de time in de world, my good man. It's a beautiful day for a visit, is it not?"

"It is," Ted agreed, squinting up at where fat clouds bobbed along in the sky and a breeze rustled the leaves of the palms overhead. Ted pulled a cooler, two chairs, and a satchel from the back of the truck while Jolie watched with an eyebrow raised. It appeared they were settling in for a while.

"Ah, you come prepared. Dis here a smart man, Jolie."

Prince nodded to Jolie and she moved to hold the gate open for Ted.

"I did tell him how engaging your stories are, Prince. I think he wants to hear for himself."

"She flatter an old man." Prince laughed and held a hand to his wiry chest. "But I never turn down de compliments of a beautiful woman."

"I've brought some coffee and some food. Can I interest you in anything?" Ted asked, as polite as any waiter at a restaurant.

"Yes, please. Jolie, you get de cups."

"Sure," Jolie said, and scampered inside to rummage in the cupboards for coffee cups and a few plates. Returning, she placed them on a weathered wood table, the flecks of paint and mismatched crockery only adding to the charm of the moment. Ted poured coffee from his thermos into the mugs and unpacked a neatly arranged plate of fruit and a small tin of chocolates. Jolie bit back a smile when Prince pulled a flask from his pocket and offered a pour for their coffees.

"Ah – no, thank you," Ted said.

"Suit yourself." Prince shrugged and poured a healthy dollop in his coffee cup. Screwing the lid back on, he leaned back, stretched his bare feet in front of him, and let out a contented sigh. "Dis here is de life, you know, man? De ocean, de sunshine, good company... what more can you ask for?"

"Not much." Ted smiled and sipped his coffee, his eyes drawn back to the water. He seemed to be in no rush to push Prince to talk, so Jolie settled in to enjoy the morning and practice being patient.

"What else you bring me?" Prince asked.

Jolie looked at him, surprised at his bluntness. Well, not really – that was his way – but this was even more blunt than he usually was.

"Prince! He's already brought you coffee and breakfast."

"Yes, I know dat, Miss Jolie. But he got something else to be showing me. I sense it," Prince said, touching a finger to his forehead and grinning widely at Jolie.

"He's not wrong," Ted said, and he leaned back in his chair to grab the strap of his knapsack. Pulling it onto his lap, he dug inside until he pulled out a blue velvet bag.

"What is it?" Jolie asked as Ted pulled an object from the bag and began unwrapping the tissue paper that surrounded it.

"I have my own mermaid artifact," Ted said, glancing at her briefly before his gaze darted away and back to the object in his hand.

"Do you? Let me see dat!" Prince exclaimed, almost bouncing right out of his seat in his excitement. Ted handed the object over and Jolie stood, leaning over Prince to look. Her stomach did a weird little flip and it took her a moment to catch her breath.

He'd found her comb.

She'd lost it. Years and years ago. It had been her favorite comb, passed down to her by Irma, and she'd worn it every full moon for their ritual. Carved from a pearly pink shell, the comb was etched with an intricate design of a mermaid embracing her man, stars and moons swirling around the two. It was deeply powerful, made with love, and Jolie had been distraught when it had been lost.

But here it was, after all these years, in the hands of the man who was her future.

"Where..." Jolie began, but her voice was a croak. She cleared her throat and tried again. "Where did you find that?" Her hands itched to snatch it away from Prince. Instead, she sat back down and took a trembling sip of her coffee.

"Every summer, my parents would try to take a week or two in Cape Cod if they could find a good vacation rental house. I carried on that tradition as an adult, and I found it on the beach early one morning. It was just sticking up from the sand, and it... hmm, I don't know how to say this, but –"

"It called to you," Prince finished, turning the comb over in his hand.

"It did. There was nobody else on the beach that morning and I was drawn to the water's edge. It pulled me. I don't know how to explain it."

"Why do you think it's a mermaid artifact?" Jolie blurted out.

"Well, for one, the drawings on it. Two, it seems to have – I don't know if I have the right words – a pulse of its own? Energy of its own? There's something there that I don't feel when I touch other hair combs, or other items, really. In fact, the only other time I've felt it was when I held Prince's shell." Ted shrugged, and Jolie studied his face. He recited the facts so coolly, almost detached, and she wondered how or what he really felt when he held the comb. Prince was right – mermaid magick worked differently for each person.

"Oh, it's mermaid, for sure," Prince confirmed, turning the comb over in his hands.

"May I?" Jolie asked, and Prince handed it over. As soon as the comb was back in her hands, it hummed in happiness. Without thinking, Jolie tucked it into her hair, just above her ear.

"Oh, it's beautiful on you," Ted said, admiring the comb.

"I'm sorry. I'm not sure why I did that," Jolie said, and reached up to pull it out. It wasn't hers anymore, Jolie reminded herself. She handed it back to Ted, though it bothered her to see it go.

Prince nodded, sipping his coffee. "It's de pull of de mermaid. It looked just right in your hair, Miss Jolie."

How had her comb made it from Siren Island all the way to Cape Cod? Jolie had searched for it often. It wasn't typical for mermaids to lose things, particularly an item of great personal meaning. For it to have traveled so far was… well, she was having a hard time understanding how it had happened.

"This comb is what inspired me to teach," Ted said, turning it over in his hands.

"Really?" Jolie asked.

"Really. I was having one of those walks where – well, I was having a crisis of self, I suppose. My investments had paid off, and my future sort of stretched before me. I didn't know what I wanted to focus on or where to put my energies. I just knew I wasn't built for a life of leisure."

"No lounging around on yachts for you?" Jolie teased.

"No, not unless the yachts were headed to some far-away and rarely traveled spot. I just… I like to keep busy. I have a busy mind and I don't think I would have been satisfied to just sit back and let life flow around me."

Prince nodded. "Like a pebble in a stream."

"Exactly. You divert the flow, but eventually the water wears you down," Ted said, taking a drink from his cup and looking back out to the water. "Finding this comb made me head to the library to research it. It just pulled me in. I don't know…the power of it or something? When I couldn't find anything about the design or the history, I delved deeper. And that's what really kicked off my passion for mermaid mythology. Once I was in, I was all the way in. That turned into a deeper dive into literature, and teaching naturally flowed from that."

"All from finding a comb?"

"It's not just any comb, Jolie. It's a mermaid comb." Prince shook his head and made a clucking sound with his mouth. "You know how powerful dese things be."

Jolie reached for the fruit bowl and popped a grape into her mouth. She decided not to say anything, just let the men hash it out while her mind churned furiously. The comb had made its way to Ted, and it had diverted his life completely. All so his passion would bring him to her doorstep. The oracle had been right: This was the man for her.

Now she only had to convince him of that.

"Why do you think they wear the combs? For adorn-ment only? Does it maybe symbolize a hierarchy in their class system?" Ted mused.

Jolie snapped back to the conversation. "For rituals."

"Rituals? What kind of rituals? That's an interesting take on it," Ted mused, holding the comb back up to the light of the sun. "What kind of rituals would a mermaid have?"

"Dey definitely have a full moon ritual," Prince said, rocking forward on his seat to take a piece of chocolate.

"Have you seen a full moon ritual?" Ted asked. "What would the purpose be?"

Prince darted a glance at Jolie, but realized she wasn't going to speak. He popped the chocolate into his mouth and hummed a bit as he thought about the question.

"Okay, dis here just what I think. I think de mermaids be ruled by de moon goddess and when she is full, dey honor her. You know how de moon pulls de ocean tides? It's all mixed together." Prince made a swirling motion with his hand as though he was stirring a stew.

"Sure – so the moon pulls the tides, and mermaids live in the water: Moon worship would be normal. It's not uncommon; many societies have full moon rituals, to mark the passage of time and so on. I'm not sure what mermaids would use for calendars, but I doubt it's an iPad app."

"You go out on de boat on de full moon here, and you'll see a mermaid." Prince nodded toward the water. "It's a breathtaking sight."

"You've seen them? You've really seen them?" Ted pulled his little recorder from his pocket. "Might I record this?"

"Sure, why not? You either believe or you don't believe." Prince shrugged, grabbing another bit of chocolate and glancing at Jolie in question.

"Tell him your stories, Prince. He's here to learn," Jolie

encouraged him. Prince had long ago figured out what they were. He was one of the few people on island that Jolie never worried about. Prince had a 'live and let live' type of attitude. He admired the mermaids, loved telling stories about them, but he'd never try to capture one. He was an ally to the mermaids, and as such, was always rewarded with bountiful hauls on the days he still fished. It was an understanding years in the making, and one Prince deeply treasured.

"Well... de first time, I 'bout fell out de boat." Prince laughed, slapping his leg. "You think you're going crazy, you know? Long days alone on de water make you question what you see. Sometimes it gets boring, so you start making up games to pass de time. Or you let your mind wander away for a while until you get de tug on your line. I was doing dat de first time, letting my mind wander. I saw de tail first, just a flip of it at de surface of de water."

"What time of day was this?" Ted asked.

"Ah, it was just coming on light. I like to go out real early in de morning. I thought maybe it was a trick of de eye – you know how things get fuzzy right before sunrise?"

"Yes, like you're looking through a haze until the sun comes up."

"Yeah, like dat. So I think to myself, huh, maybe dis is just a whale – we have dem, you know – like maybe a small pilot whale. Or a dolphin. You see dem farther out and all. So I'm curious and I go a little farther forward."

"What happened?"

"She popped her head up and smiled at me! I almost fell out de boat, I swear to you. I thought, dat's it, Prince.

You've finally gone and lost it. I always thought maybe I'd go crazy one of dese days, sitting out on de boat for hours talking to myself. And here it finally happens; I'm hallucinating."

"Did she speak to you? What did she look like?"

"She only smiled. Swam right up to de boat and pulled herself up to look at me." Prince shivered as he remembered. "I thought she would kill me."

"Why?"

"Because legends say sirens can be as deadly as dey are friendly."

"What did you do?"

"I offered her de fish I had. Said I was sorry if I was hurting the ocean, but I was only a simple fisherman trying to feed my family. She laughed at me, shook her head, and disappeared."

"What did she look like?"

"Oh, beauty beyond words. Like dis one." Prince tilted his head at Jolie and she held her breath when Ted turned to study her. Would he compliment her again? "Long flowing hair, a beautiful face, and just… a glow to her. You could feel her power."

"I understand that," Ted muttered and Jolie raised an eyebrow. What did that mean, exactly?

"But she meant me no harm. I guess she was just checking me out. Making sure I wasn't doing anything wrong."

"What do you think would be considered wrong?"

"You know, de usual – trying to catch sharks for de fins, or capture dolphins. Nasty stuff people do."

"But fishing is okay?"

"Sustainable fishing is," Jolie murmured.

"Ah, I suppose."

"There's a big difference between commercial fleets taking out entire populations of fish and local fisherman taking in a small haul to feed their families and sell a few on the market," Jolie explained, finishing her coffee and setting the cup on the table.

"So mermaids are conservationists then?"

"Yes." Prince nodded solemnly. "Dey have to be. It's their home."

CHAPTER 16

"Was that your only encounter?" Ted asked. Then he laughed, running his hands over his face. "Not that I'm downplaying that particular meeting. But if you have more, I'd love to hear."

"Many of us do. Dey choose, you see? Dey choose when dey feel like showing demselves." Prince nodded solemnly. "Always a gift, it is."

"Of course. It sounds like the best gift in the world to me," Ted said with a laugh. "I think I'd be beaming for weeks if that were to happen to me."

"You'll see dem. Trust," Prince said, tapping a weathered hand to his chest. "Trust in here."

"Ah, well – who's to say, really? I'm just happy to meet someone with a firsthand account."

"I've seen dem since then. Time to time."

"Do they ever speak to you?"

"You can hear dem singing, you know. Late at night. It's enough to make you want to walk straight into de water. A siren's song – it's mighty powerful."

"How do you stop yourself from going in the water?"

"I don't think dey want you to go in. I think if dey want you to walk into de water, dere's nothing you can do to resist. When you hear dem sing, dat's dem blessing you with a song. With love. Dey protect dis island. It's a blessing, man, a blessing through and through."

"Fascinating," Ted murmured. "How does one go about hearing them? Or seeing them? Do you truly think if I go to the water on a full moon I might see them? Or if I go out early in the morning?"

"I don't know about de times of de night, I really don't. I think you could go out to de water every day for de rest of your life – if dey don't want to be seen, you ain't gonna see dem."

"So, why you then?" Ted asked.

Prince threw his head back and roared with laughter. "Why a poor grizzled old man like me, you thinking? Not some fancy yacht captain?"

"No…" Ted's cheeks tinged that pink color again. "I wasn't implying you weren't worthy of their gift or anything of the sort. I'm just trying to learn, and I wonder why you think they trusted you versus, say, your neighbor down the road."

"My neighbor down de road seen dem too." Prince slapped his knee and chortled.

"Is that so? Would they be willing to speak to me?"

"I can't speak for dem. But you come to de party dis week and you can ask yourself."

"What party?"

"We have a meetup on Fridays. Come pass by for a beer or two."

"What's the address?" Ted asked, pulling a pen and notebook from his pocket.

Prince slapped his knee and laughed once again. "Everyone know where it be. Jolie will bring you. Won't you?" Prince turned to her and she nodded.

"Thank you for the invitation. That's very welcoming of you," Ted said.

"Listen to dis one." Prince turned to look at Jolie. "He's nice. Not like some of de others you bring around."

"I can't control what guests we have stay with us." Jolie smiled.

"He's smart, but don't talk down to me. He don't make fun of my stories. He's listening. Dis here's a good one."

"Duly noted."

"Now, Ted. To answer your question – I don't know why me. I think, maybe, b'cause I really love de island. And de ocean. I respect de ocean more than anything. She's a moody one, she is. Moody and miraculous, all in one. Only someone who can love de sea like dat... well, maybe dat's de gift in return. De mermaids can read my heart."

"That's enchanting." Ted nodded along with Prince's words. "And makes perfect sense. It's a great gift you've been given."

"Don't I know it?" Prince stood. "Now, it's time for me to visit my Maria. She fusses, you know."

"Thank you for your time today, Prince. And for the invitation. I'll be delighted to join your party. Is there anything I can bring for the table?"

"Oh, listen to dis one. I like him, Jolie." Prince laughed and patted her shoulder as he passed her, disappearing into his house. It seemed their morning coffee time was over.

"That's a no, then?" Ted asked, looking after him.

"We won't go empty-handed," Jolie promised him. "We can bring something to drink. Knowing Irma, she'll whip up a dessert or something to be passed around. It's not fancy," Jolie warned.

"I wasn't expecting fancy," Ted promised. "But I do want to make sure I'm being polite."

"I don't think you're in any danger of giving the wrong impression."

"So long as I don't kick any babies between now and then, I should be good," Ted said.

Jolie found herself snorting again. She slapped a hand over her face and glared at Ted over her fingers. "You have to stop that."

"What? Making you snort? I think that's going to be my mission from now on. I won't be pleased with my day if I haven't had at least one charming Jolie-snort."

"Can we stop saying that? Even the sound of the word is indelicate."

"Snort? Snort. Snort. Snooooort. Snnnnooooort," Ted repeated in different intonations until Jolie threw up her hands and laughed. She collected the cups and took them into Prince's house to wash and leave on the drying rack. Coming back outside, she found Ted leaning against the wall in the shade of the tree and staring out to sea.

"Do you believe him?" Ted asked, not looking at Jolie.

"Of course," Jolie said, tilting her head to look up at Ted.

"No hesitation? No questions asked?"

"I've known Prince my entire life. He's never once lied to me. Irma trusts him, and her bullshit detector is spot-on. Plus, I believe in mermaids. I've seen them too."

"Have you really?"

"I told you that."

"I'd like to get your story."

"I'll tell you. I promise. But not yet."

At that, Ted shifted his gaze to look down on her. They were so close their arms almost touched, and Jolie could swear she felt electricity zipping between their bodies.

"Why not yet?"

"I'll know when it's time. I'd like to tell it when I'm ready."

"Now you have me very curious."

"I don't doubt it. But you have more research to do, boss-man, and I'll wait until you compile most of it before adding my own data points to it."

"Wow, day one on the job and you've already got the lingo down."

"Thank you." Jolie fake-curtsied, and then laughed up at him. "Okay, boss-man. Where to next?"

"I heard something about cave drawings?"

"Ah, yes. A fine choice for your next adventure. I really love your comb, by the way. It's – well, it's very powerful."

"You felt that too?" Ted asked, then looked at her when he realized he had just admitted he'd felt the comb's power.

"Naturally. I can tell you more about that comb, as well, if you'd like."

"I'd love to know more."

"Come on then, I'll tell you at the caves. First, though, you need more sunscreen." Jolie pulled a tube from her pocket and squirted it on her hands. Before she could think too long about it, she cupped his face in her hands and began to stroke the cream across his face. They stood there, sunglasses shading their eyes, and the moment drew out between them as Jolie worked the lotion into his skin.

"Thank you," Ted said, stepping back.

"Um, you're welcome. Sorry about doing that without asking. People just forget to reapply here and then their trip gets ruined by the burns."

"It was nice of you. Like a mother hen looking out for her chicks," Ted said, holding the gate to the garden for her.

Jolie flounced out, turning her head so he wouldn't see her face. A mother hen? As *if*.

This whole patience thing was going to take, well, some patience.

CHAPTER 17

"So, I take it these will be Indian rock drawings?" Ted asked once they were back in the truck. "I wonder how far they date back to."

"We do have Indian rock drawings here as well. The Arawak Indians have a rich history on the island. But these are mermaid etchings, not Indian ones."

"How do you know the difference?"

"I…" Jolie trailed off as she thought about how to explain her reasoning in a way that wasn't just 'because I said so' and actually held merit. "The Arawak drawings are sort of a faded orangey color -- mainly, I suspect, from tar or other dark inks that stained the rock. But the mermaid etchings are actual carvings into the rock; they would have been quite difficult to do with the tools the Arawaks had at the time. Or at the very least, incredibly labor intensive."

"Interesting. You don't think the etchings could have been passed down through the generations, with each family contributing to them?"

"Perhaps, but I'm going to go with mermaid."

"So... just like the statue showing up out of the blue?"

"Pretty much." Jolie glanced at him to see a smile hovering on his face. "What's that look for?"

"It's just nice to be around someone who has such a casual acceptance of magick. If I was talking about this back home, I'd have to fight for every inch of leverage in a conversation. Here, I can speak with people who just easily accept that there are some things in this world that can't be explained. It's nice."

"But I already gave you an explanation – magick."

"Right, right," Ted said, and Jolie realized that while he was quite open-minded, Ted wasn't really ready to fully embrace all the mystic things that surrounded the myths of the mermaids. It made sense, she thought as she directed him off the main road and down a craggy dirt track. Magick was the norm for her. She'd never *not* known it. For someone uninitiated, it would be harder to embrace. So points to Ted for trying to understand and for not belittling her beliefs. It took a strong person to accept someone else's beliefs while not fully comprehending or supporting them. He wasn't telling her she was wrong; he just didn't agree with the same things she did. Yet.

"I'm sorry. I'm not trying to say you're a liar," Ted said, snapping Jolie out of her thoughts.

"No, I didn't take it that way. It's new for you, this concept of magick, yes?"

"Well, I mean, I've certainly read about it. But, yes, relatively new in the sense of meeting people who accept magick as an unequivocal answer for unexplainable things."

"There is an explanation though," Jolie said gently. "As I've already said. Magick."

"Got it," Ted said, a ghost of a smile on his lips. "You're very kindly telling me to eff off."

"I would be if I thought you were being rude or mean. It's just not something you've had exposure to, is all. Let me ask you this: Do you believe in mermaids? Truly?"

"Listen," Ted said as he downshifted to trundle the truck over a particularly rocky bit in the road, "I want to believe. I really, really, really want to believe."

"Ah, but you're not yet there. You can't truly say, 'I believe in mermaids.'"

"I believe that others believe in them."

"That's a small step in the right direction. But you held the comb and felt something. You held the shell and felt something. How do you explain that?"

"Intuition?" Ted asked, slowing the truck further as the path became more overgrown. Jolie rolled up her window against the prickly branches of the brush that slapped against the sides of the truck.

"Okay, that's a start. But what would you be intuiting then?"

"Um… that there's energy I can't explain around these objects."

"Well, we have some work for you to do, Dr. Macalister. Maybe I'll need to assign you some homework," Jolie mused. The road forked, and she pointed to the right.

"I look forward to it. I'm not saying you're wrong. I'm open to learning."

"And that's a very admirable trait. Not many have it."

"I think the road is running out," Ted said, pulling the truck to a stop by a rocky beach.

"Actually, if you pull around those boulders, you can go a little further. But it looks like the tide is coming in, so best to stay here."

They'd arrived at a rocky shoreline where the water hugged an outcropping of cliffs. The midday sun bore down on them as they left the truck, and Jolie tipped her face to it. She always enjoyed the sun; it felt like she was absorbing energy from dancing rays of light. It was a different energy than the moon's, but both were rejuvenating for her. A gull swooped lazily overhead, turning its head to eye them, curious as to why they were tromping along her shoreline.

"And now I defer to you, O mighty research assistant. You may lead the way," Ted said with a gesture, putting on a hat to shade his face. She imagined he had all sorts of necessary items in the pack slung on his back; he didn't strike her as someone who was often unprepared.

"Follow me, boss," Jolie teased, and almost grabbed his hand to tug him after her. Reminding herself of their business relationship, she let her hand drop and instead trained her eyes on her feet – it was a tricky path to pick their way through. They wandered along the beach, stepping over craggy rocks and through tidal pools with crabs skittering about, before they reached the cliff that jutted out into the water. There, Jolie stopped and turned back to Ted.

"Your feet will get wet here. There's a small ledge that runs the length of the cliff just under the water. It's only about a foot wide, so you'll want to hug the cliff wall and stick to it. Otherwise you can twist an ankle or fall into the water."

"Understood," Ted said, reaching out to place a hand on the rocky wall, his eyes intent on his feet. Trusting he would follow her instructions, Jolie breezed across the path to the hidden sandy beach on the other side of the cliff. Ted followed quickly, and she was pleased to see he hadn't had a mishap. Though, once again, there was a part of her that wished to see him flustered – if not by her, then by anything, really. Nobody could be this perfect.

Not everyone would think he is perfect, Jolie reminded herself, turning away as her face heated. It was her own crush talking.

"This place is incredible. It looks like it should be in a travel magazine in an article about hidden paradises or off-the-beaten-path locales. I'm surprised it's not teeming with people."

"Mmm, I think many of the locals prefer the more easily-accessible beaches. Or places that have a tiki bar and a bathroom." Jolie laughed, slipping her shoes off to let them dry – and so she could dig her toes into the sand. There was nothing like the feel of warm sand under her toes, and even though it burned slightly from the midday sun, she didn't care. Rooting herself to the beach, she let the energy of the earth pulse lightly through her, calming her racing heart and helping her to refocus on their task. And not on the fact that she wanted to pull the delightful Dr. Macalister to the sand and show him the pleasures of her own hidden paradise.

"I suppose. This is authentic, though. It's really stunning. And untouched. Just look at these cliffs! I could spend hours exploring here. Or bring a hammock and read for days," Ted said, turning around in a circle to appreciate the beach.

"We could come camp here one night if you'd like."

"Really?" Ted turned to look at her with a wide smile.

"Of course. Why not?"

"Why not, indeed? I don't suppose you have to reserve a campground or get permission, do you?"

"From whom? It's an abandoned beach." Jolie laughed. "Come on, I'll show you the etchings."

"Even if I never saw anything mermaid-related here, this is a real treat. Thank you for bringing me, Jolie."

"Hey, you're paying me. Just trying to make my first day on the job a memorable one."

"You're winning employee of the month, I can promise you that."

"Yes! My first business award." Jolie shot him a grin over her shoulder, then led him to a tangled mess of bushes with a few particularly gnarly cactuses growing about. "Now, most people would stop here because, well, thorns are unpleasant. But if you skirt the bushes and turn at that large cactus…" Jolie trailed off as Ted followed her around the brush and to where a small path became apparent.

"Oh, sneaky. I never would have seen that from the beach," Ted said, his body close to hers. Jolie wondered if he could feel the energy that snapped between them when they stood close.

"That's likely by design. Follow me. Oh, do you have a flashlight?"

"I do." *Of course*, he did.

"Great, we're going into a little cave of sorts. You aren't claustrophobic?"

"Nope, all good there."

"Let's go, then," Jolie said and ducked into a small opening in the rocky outcrop, then turned her body sideways to slide through a narrow passage. Her eyes adjusted to the dark instantly, but she didn't want to tell Ted that. "I'll take that light when you have a chance."

"Of course," Ted said, clicking it on.

Light flooded around her. Glancing back, she put up a hand to shield her eyes and saw him with a camping light on his head. Naturally.

"It's not too far up – this particular cave doesn't connect to any of the larger caverns."

"Are there a lot of cave systems on the island?"

"Yes, quite a few. Some still undiscovered, I'm sure. But we do have a bat population and you can book a tour to visit their natural habitat as well."

"I might do that."

"Here," Jolie said, stopping just as the path widened into a small room. On one wall, an intricate carving into the rockface stood out in dark relief against the grey color of the stone.

"What…" Ted's hands came to her shoulders as he studied the carving. For a moment, Jolie allowed herself to lean back against him, enjoying the warmth of his broad chest at her back. Closing her eyes, she breathed in the scent of him – sunscreen mixed with soap – and hoped he would stand there a little bit longer as she tried to memorize the feel of his body against her.

"Jolie, this is fascinating. I haven't seen anything like

this mentioned here or anyone talking about it," Ted breathed, moving around her to crouch in front of it. He brought his hand up to touch it; then, thinking better of it, he let his hand drop as he studied the carving.

The carving depicted a series of events. In the first, a mermaid swam beside a boat. The next was of a mermaid and human entwined while waves crashed around them – the same carving on the comb that Ted had tucked in his pack. The third showed a mermaid in the water, her hands reaching out to a man out of reach on the beach. Over it all, the moon goddess Selene shone down upon them. Below, an underwater mermaid village was depicted among the seagrasses and corals where sea life were friends, and mermaids lived in harmony.

"Nobody really knows about it. It's been kept secret for a reason." Jolie decided to leave out the tidbit of it being protected by magick. Only certain people were allowed to enter, which was why most people never discovered the path to the cave.

"You think people would vandalize this?"

"I think sometimes people can be stupid. Or kids may think they're being cool. It's better this way."

"I suppose you'd be against me taking a picture of this?"

Jolie hesitated, then said, "Yes, actually I would." She also didn't want to explain to him why his pictures would never show up, no matter how many he took. The carving was something to experience solely in the moment.

"Maybe I could sketch it," Ted said, his voice at a whisper as he studied the carving. "You're right. This is incredible work; Indians with primitive tools would have had difficulty achieving this effect. I can't help but wonder if there's a master artist on the island who snuck in here and did this."

"It's been around for ages," Jolie said, leaning back against the wall to study him. "This is not a recent thing."

"No, I don't suppose it is," Ted mused, leaning forward to study the moss growing in some of the grooves. "Is that...?"

"The same depiction as on your comb? Yes."

"Oh," Ted said, his head snapping back as he turned to look at Jolie. "That can't be a coincidence."

"No, not likely."

"How in the world could this design be on the wall here and on a comb that washed up on the beach in Cape Cod?" Ted asked, and pulled the comb out of his bag to hold it up to compare with the wall etching. "There's no way this is mass produced. It's not like some plastic mold where these designs get stamped out."

"Nope," Jolie agreed, crossing her legs and watching Ted as he tried to think of all the ways this couldn't be the magick of mermaids.

"They're remarkably similar. The carvings, I mean. Down to the curl of the mermaid's hair." Ted held up the comb again and looked between the two scenes depicting the mermaid and her lover.

"Remarkable," Jolie said.

"So, a secret mermaid cave and a drawing on Siren Island is replicated on a supposed mermaid comb that washed up at my feet in Cape Cod. How is this possible?"

"Who's to say, really?" Jolie said, putting a breezy note in her voice as she dug a hole in the sand with her toe.

"You're telling me this is magick."

"I'm not saying anything." Jolie held up her hands. "I'm just the assistant, remember? I'll leave you to draw your own conclusions."

"But there's no way something like this could happen. It's... there's just... it can't..." Ted's gaze bounced between the comb and the carving.

"Okay, if you suspended all judgment, what is your gut telling you about this? First thing that pops in your head," Jolie said, coming to crouch next to him and meeting his eyes.

"That I was meant to come here. For some reason. The comb was a sign."

Pleased, Jolie reached out and squeezed his arm. The man wasn't a total loss, she realized.

"Indeed."

"But that doesn't make sense."

"Why do you think magick has to be logical?"

"I... oh gosh, I can't even begin to pick that apart. I'm still tripping over the fact that these two designs match."

"Best just to sit with that, then."

"But if I'm meant to come here... why? To write my paper? I don't get it..." Ted shook his head while Jolie looked at him silently and willed him to see her. When nothing more came, she sighed and stood up.

"Maybe it's a clue. You'll figure it out in time. Just be patient." Jolie winced as she said it, but it was the truth. He was closer to being ready to see her for what she really was than she was to being vulnerable to him.

CHAPTER 18

*T*he woman walked out of the water, much like Jolie had that first day, making his breath hitch as he watched her. Ted crouched at the shoreline, the moon bathing the beach with her gentle light, as the naked woman approached him. Her skin, slick with saltwater, glistened in the light and her hair ran in sleek waves over her back. She was everywoman – both ethereal and robust – and he dropped to his knees to offer his worship.

"Man." Her voice cascaded across his skin, sending shivers through his body and making the tiny hairs at the back of his neck stand on end. "Why do you bow to me?"

"I believe you are a goddess, and thus it is respectful," Ted said immediately, not daring to look her in the eye.

"Stand before me."

Ted stood, his eyes glancing across her naked breasts, and darting up to her eyes. It wouldn't be wise to ogle a goddess, not if he was trying to be polite.

"Why have you come here?"

"Um, for a vacation. And to learn about the mermaids,

of course. It's a passion of mine, you see…" Ted trailed off when he realized he was babbling.

"You find us passionate?" The mermaid's eyes held his and his body hummed with lust. *She* was doing that, he realized – making him want her.

"I… no, I meant I have a passion for learning about mermaids. I find you fascinating," Ted explained, sweat breaking out across his brow.

"What fascinates you about us, man? You like our bodies? You think we will be good lovers for you?"

Oh god. Ted had a flash of tangled limbs and hours of pleasure at the hands of this goddess and heat shot through his entire body.

"No. I mean, yes, but no."

"Speak sense to me."

"I… what I mean to say is that I think the myths and legends about your kind are fascinating. For centuries now, every seafaring culture across the world has had some tale of encounters with mermaids. It's… enchanting, is all."

"Do you mean us harm?"

"What? No, of course not. I mean no harm. I'm a student, really. A student of the world. I just like to learn. I would never harm your kind."

"You mean no harm. And yet you turn your back on what is in front of you."

"Hmmm." Ted didn't know how to answer that, but his mind flashed to Jolie.

"Why are you worthy of our trust?"

"Your trust? Well, I think because I respect you – well, really, I try to respect all cultures. I want to learn, but not exploit. If it came down to it, I'd throw my research away to protect what I find."

"Would you protect me?" The goddess stepped forward and trailed her finger across Ted's cheek and over his lips. "If it were to come to it? Would you?"

"Of course," Ted breathed, stunned at her closeness. Power emanated from her in sharp waves, and there was no questioning that he was in the presence of greatness.

"I see by your eyes that is true. And yet..."

"Yet?"

"You still don't believe, do you?"

"I want to." Ted was shocked to feel tears sheen his eyes. "I want to so desperately. But... I can't. I think I need to see to believe. I'm sorry I can't take this on faith alone. Maybe I'm too pragmatic. Maybe I'm just wishing for the miracle. I just – I'm sorry. I don't mean to hurt you."

"You don't hurt me, man. Many don't believe. We prefer it that way. It protects our society. But you are hurting someone else."

"Who? Why? What can I do?"

"You need to look at what's right in front of you."

"You're right in front of me," Ted pointed out.

The goddess threw back her head and laughed. "Oh, I like you. It's not often a human will make me laugh. You, man, need to see what is in front of you. Not from here..." The goddess traced his eyes, and then brought her hand to his chest. "But from in here."

"I'm sorry. I wish I could understand what you mean."

"You will. In time. For now, because you've made me laugh, I'll leave you with a gift."

"A gift?" Ted watched as she took a necklace from around her neck – his eyes hovering for only a second on her breasts, which he considered a win – and handed it to him. Ted held it up to the light. Cowrie shells separated by small turquoise beads led down to a mother-of-pearl pendant. In the pendant, a mermaid and a man were wrapped around each other. "Is this the same etching as on the comb I found?"

"It is. We don't give these gifts lightly. Each contains power. You feel it, don't you?" The goddess touched his chest. "You feel the power?"

"I do, yes."

"Good. You are worthy of such a gift. It's not meant for you to keep, though."

"Who is it for?"

"You'll know."

"What will it mean? Shouldn't I keep it as a set, with the comb?"

"Listen to your intuition. I must go – Mother Moon is calling me home."

"But wait – who is this meant for?" Ted asked.

The goddess only shot him a look over her shoulder before walking into the dark water and slipping beneath the surface.

Looking down at the necklace in his hands, Ted couldn't deny the power that thrummed through him. If only he could understand the meaning...

When he woke in the morning, Ted pushed himself up on the bed and squinted at the early morning light shining gently through the sheer curtains of the window. Outside, the waves crashed against the shore and he could hear the cries of the gulls looking for their breakfast. Sitting up, Ted went to run a hand through his hair, his mind on the vivid dream he'd had. When something in his hand slapped him in the face, he looked down in shock.

There, entwined in his fingers, was the necklace from his dream the night before.

CHAPTER 19

"Where's Sam?" Jolie asked, strolling in the garden behind Lola's store, Mirra at her heels.

"Ah, she's being Sam. I swear, you'd think she'd settle down and go at a relaxed pace since she's moved here, but she's busier than ever." Lola walked into the garden carrying a tray with a red teapot that had hand-painted flowers on it and a plate piled high with cookies. It was their weekly teatime date, something that had evolved naturally into a routine. It was nice to carve out a moment of girl time each week to talk about everything – or nothing at all. Periodically, Irma would drop in, or their new friend Avery. Sometimes Prince's Maria would wander through and cluck over them, making sure everyone was eating and drinking enough. There were no formal invites, but it was understood that anyone was welcome – even one of the men, if they bothered to drop in.

"I don't think the concept of slowing down has ever

really entered her mind. Being busy seems to soothe her in a weird way," Mirra said, plopping onto a wicker chair with a bright blue cushion. She'd braided her blond hair back and piled it on her head due to the heat, and she wore a loose blush-pink dress that floated around her like a cloud. Jolie had gone for screaming red in a dress that ended at mid-thigh, and gold bracelets stacked on her wrists. She, too, had wound her hair up on top of her head, and gold aviators shielded her eyes from the sun. Some might think the way she dressed was too fancy for the island, but Jolie rarely cared what people thought of her. Bodies were meant to be adorned – why not do so in a lovely manner?

"Jolie, you look decadent," Lola said, studying Jolie as she sat on a bench by the table and pulled her feet under her. The garden behind Lola's shop had been transformed into a mixed-use space where people could grab a cup of coffee, spend time painting, or meet for the wine-and-paint class Lola held each week. Palm trees shaded the garden, and pots of hibiscus and other tropical flowers were scattered amidst mismatched chairs, loungers, and squat garden stools and tables. Lanterns, sourced from all over the world, dotted the tables and hung from the trees; at night everything was lit up, making the space look like a colorful fairy garden.

"Obviously not decadent enough for some people," Jolie said, annoyed at the petulant tone that crept into her voice.

"Ah." Lola looked to Mirra who nodded back at her.

"He hasn't paid her any attention," Mirra said, reaching out to stroke Jolie's arm.

"I find that very hard to believe. You're about as impossible to ignore as a shard of glass in your foot." Lola shook her head as she poured their tea, then winced. "Sorry, that probably wasn't the best analogy."

"You're right, though. Jolie is a powerhouse. It's rare that a man isn't distracted or attracted. He's holding strong, this one," Mirra said.

"I'm his *employee*. I never should have accepted the job. Now he'll never look at me as anything more. I swear, the man is straight as an arrow. No dallying with colleagues, not even any flirtation. Even when he does compliment me, he does it in such a sterile way that it might as well be my grandfather saying it."

"Sounds like he's a good man," Lola said, then leaned back when Jolie glared at her.

"She's a bit touchy today. I don't think she slept well," Mirra whispered loudly across the table.

"I know he's a good man."

"But, really, Jolie. I mean a good *good* man. When you meet someone who treats relationship boundaries seriously and is respectful of you, that speaks a lot about his core values. This isn't a man you'd have to worry about – like who he's texting on the phone or where he is late at night. He'll always be straight with you. It's remarkably refreshing to be with someone like that."

"But I'm *not* with him. I *can't* be with him because he won't see me," Jolie said, grabbing a cookie from the plate and taking a sullen bite. Times like these called for choco-late. A lot of it.

"He sees you, Jolie. I thought we talked about being

patient? It's been, what, like a couple days?" Lola tucked a wayward curl under her sparkly headband.

"It has come to my understanding that patience is not an area in which I excel," Jolie said, and the other women let out peals of laughter.

"Duh," Mirra said, and grabbed a cookie while Jolie glared at her.

"Ah, isn't dis de prettiest picture on de island! Have I died and gone to heaven?" Prince asked, wandering into the garden. Lola hopped up to give him a kiss on the cheek before going inside to procure another cup. Prince pulled up a stool, not having to be invited, and leaned over to take a cookie from the pile on the table.

"You just might have, Prince. I've told you time and again – we're goddesses." Jolie smiled at him.

"Don't I know it? But I'll tell you all a secret." Prince leaned in as Lola returned with a cup and poured his tea.

"What's the secret, Prince?"

"All women are goddesses. Not just de fancy ones like you. Nothing like a woman's power. Nothing like it at all." Prince laughed and rocked back and forth on his stool.

"It would be nice if more people held your view," Jolie said, reaching over to pat Prince's arm. "You're a feminist."

"I'm probably more dan dat. My life been much better since I let Maria drive de train. I don't need to be equal with her – how could I be? It's an honor to serve."

"We need more men like you, Prince. Maybe not needing to bow to us, but at the very least not getting in our way," Mirra observed.

"Now, dat don't stop me wanting to meddle in certain

affairs though, you see," Prince said, his gaze returning to Jolie.

"And what are you being nosy about today?" Jolie already knew where he was going, but decided to let him wind his way there.

"I like your new guest. Dr. Ted. He's a nice man."

"He is," Jolie and Mirra agreed.

"Haven't met him yet," Lola said with a shrug.

"He's open, you know? He isn't trying to judge," Prince continued, leaning over to grab another cookie. Jolie couldn't blame him. Chocolate chip oatmeal cookies with a touch of cinnamon were hard to resist.

"I get that," Jolie said.

"How come he have your comb?" Prince demanded.

And there it was, Jolie thought. She'd wondered if Prince had been able to decipher her reaction to the comb.

"What comb? What happened?" Mirra and Lola looked back and forth between them.

"It seems Dr. Macalister has his own mermaid arti-fact," Jolie said. "Much like Prince's mermaid shell. But this is a comb with a very intricate carving on it. It washed ashore at Ted's feet on the beach in Cape Cod."

"Jolie," Mirra said, reaching out to grasp Jolie's arm, "is this *your* missing comb?"

"It is," Jolie confirmed as Lola looked around at them all, her pretty eyes wide with surprise. "How did you know it was my comb, Prince?"

"I see de energy now, you know? Maybe it's my old age. But I can kind of see…" Prince waved his gnarled hand in the air in a swooping motion. "Like colors or auras around things. And dat comb? It match your color. It has your energy. For sure it does."

"Jolie. You searched for ages for that comb," Mirra whispered. "How in the world could it have traveled so far?"

"I think it was meant to bring him here."

"You like him, don't you?" Prince asked, his face falling into crinkles as he smiled at Jolie. "Is dis de one?"

"I like him. And, yes. But he doesn't see that."

"Never stopped you before."

"It's different this time."

"So? You're a goddess. Use your goddess ways. What man could resist?" Prince stood up as though the matter was solved. "You dance with him tonight. You'll get in his brain. Trust me."

"If only it were so easy."

"Easier dan you think. Dat's de trouble dese days. Too many people overthinking things." With that, Prince whistled away, presumably going to find and serve his Maria as she set up for the party tonight.

"I'm sorry… I'm just trying to follow all this. You're saying a hair comb of yours went missing and ended up thousands of miles away at the feet of this man?" Lola asked.

"Yes. It was a special comb. Ornamental. Given to me by Irma – well, passed down through generations, really. I was distraught when it was lost. It's not often we can't find something."

"Gosh, we searched for the longest time, didn't we, Jolie? It was one of the only things we've never recovered."

"And now it's found its way home? With a very handsome man in tow." Lola looked up. "What? I've seen him. He's good-looking."

"Keep your eyes on your own man," Jolie hissed.

Lola chuckled. "I'm very happy with my man. But I can still look at the menu, can't I?"

"Have you told him about Nalachi? And the history?" Mirra asked, before Jolie's temper could rise.

"I have."

"What about the importance of gifting in mermaid culture? Does he realize that finding something like that isn't just happenstance? That gift-giving in mermaid culture holds much deeper meaning than it does for humans?"

"I personally haven't spoken with him about that, no. But that doesn't mean he hasn't uncovered it in his research."

"Breadcrumbs," Lola blurted, then laughed when they stared at her like she was one crayon short of a box.

"I'm sorry?" Mirra asked.

"You need to leave him a trail of breadcrumbs so he can find his way to you. He's been given clues for years now. But short of you dragging him into the water and changing in front of him, he's not going to get it. And, frankly, that may be too much of a shock to his system anyway. Not before he's fallen for you. You have to lead him there. Let him follow the breadcrumbs."

"I'm not getting the breadcrumb reference, but the rest makes sense."

"It's from one of the human stories – something about

a child lost in the woods and leaving a trail of breadcrumbs to find their way home," Mirra said.

"Okay, maybe not the best analogy. I'm not doing well on that front today. But basically, you need to gently lead him to you. If he's methodical, which it sounds like he is, you need to build his knowledge about mermaids, while also being open to him as a person. He's not going to fall for you overnight, and that's okay, Jolie." Lola grabbed Jolie's arm. "That's really okay. You have to hear that. Sometimes the people who fall fast into love aren't going to last long. The fire can burn too hot. It sounds like he's someone who really thinks things through. There's no reason this wouldn't apply to his approach to love. So lead him there, slowly but surely."

"I think she's right, Jolie. You'll scare him off if you try to jump him, especially now that you work for him. You need to be like a striptease, not a flasher."

"Wait, what?" Jolie said when Lola snorted with laughter.

"Woo him. Like you're doing a striptease. One small item of clothing at a time, slow and seductive. Don't just rip your dress off and show him the goods."

"She's got it," Lola agreed, leaning over to high-five Mirra.

"Striptease." Jolie mulled it over as she reached for another cookie. "Oddly enough, that makes sense."

"Practice those moves, girl." Lola did a little shimmy in place.

"Oh, I will. Starting tonight."

CHAPTER 20

She kept the red dress on. Decadent was a good description, and red was certainly her color. Jolie wound a glittery gold band into her hair, braiding it so that half of her dark hair was pulled up and the rest left to tumble down her back. Finding a lipstick that matched the color of her dress, she slicked it on her lips so they looked like a succulent cherry just waiting to be tasted. Done with makeup and hair, she put on shimmery gold sandals that laced up her legs, then stood to grab her bag. Ted wouldn't know what hit him.

But subtly, she reminded herself. Striptease. Look, but don't touch. The name of the game was to distract him and get into his brain. Even just a little bit.

Jolie met Irma and Mirra in the kitchen, where they were packing a hamper of food to bring to the party.

"What did you make?" Jolie asked.

"I was craving simple today, so I went with a crowd pleaser," Irma said and held up a see-through glass container packed full of brownies.

"You can't go wrong with chocolate."

"No, you can't. She's being stingy though, and won't let me try one," Mirra pouted.

"You look pretty," Jolie said, admiring Mirra's simple blue slip dress.

"Thank you. I'm glad you kept that dress on; I love it. Plus the gold adds a nice pop." Mirra nodded at her in approval.

"And what am I? The ugly stepsister?" Irma demanded, arms out at her sides.

Jolie cast an appraising glance over her. She'd chosen a deep purple dress, shot through with threads of silver, with intricate sequins beaded at the neckline.

"You are the grand dame. Our queen. The most stunning in all the land," Jolie promised, moving over to press a kiss to her mother's cheek. Realizing she needed more, Jolie leaned in for a hug and sighed as her mother's arms came around her and held her. In moments, her anxiety was soothed and her mood lightened. Whatever might come, her mother would be there for her. It was a bond that ran as deep as the ocean, and one Jolie was forever grateful for.

"Are you doing okay, Jolie?" Irma asked, her arms still around her daughter.

"I am. I'm shaken to my core, I won't lie. But I'm strong."

"Excuse me," Ted said, knocking at the door jamb, "I don't mean to interrupt. Should I wait outside?"

"No, please, join us. We're just packing the cooler for tonight."

"You are all a pretty sight. I wish I could paint," Ted

said, framing his fingers and holding them up to look through them. "The three of you could be cover models. If this were Renaissance times you'd each probably have a gazillion portraits of you, and artists lining up outside your door to paint you."

"Well, now, isn't that sweet?" Jolie dimpled up at him. "You look very dashing yourself."

"Oh, thank you. I wasn't sure what to wear," Ted said, glancing down at his dark grey shorts and short-sleeved button-down. Jolie drew closer to squint at the little pink dots all over his blue shirt.

"Are those flamingos?"

"They are. I thought they were festive."

About as festive as a sparkler instead of fireworks, but in his world of khaki pants, Jolie supposed small pink flamingos were a huge risk.

"They are. Now that you've got your party shirt on, are you ready to meet the locals?"

"I can't wait. I really enjoyed getting to speak with Prince. He's a great guy."

"He is. Most people dismiss him as just a poor local fisherman," Irma said as Ted picked up both the hamper and the cooler.

"He strikes me as someone who has his hands in many pots. It wouldn't surprise me if he had several businesses on the island," Ted mused.

"Ah, you're a good judge of character, Theodore. Our Prince is a bit of a mogul."

"A mogul? What kind?"

"Mainly real estate, but he dabbles elsewhere too."

"I like that about him. Low-key guy."

"It lets him read people, and move in and out of all sorts of neighborhoods easily. He's welcomed wherever he goes, and if people who are new to the island dismiss him or talk down to him – well, he won't rent or sell to them. He's very particular," Jolie said as they approached the truck.

"I'm driving tonight. You three can drink." Irma held up the keys.

"I should say no, but it might be fun to have a few drinks," Ted admitted, holding the door for Mirra, who got in the front seat.

"Wow, would you look at that? Flamingos *and* a few cocktails? Island life is getting to you." Jolie smiled her thanks up at him as he held the back door.

"I'll have you know I was considered quite a wild man at one point," Ted sniffed as he climbed in the other side of the truck.

"Is that so? Three-day parties? Strippers? Cocaine? Naughty weekends in Vegas?" Jolie asked, then slapped a hand over her mouth when she snorted at Ted's horrified look. "Damn it."

"Anything I say after that is going to sound mild now," Ted groused, and the women all laughed.

Mirra turned to look over her shoulder at him as Irma drove away from the Laughing Mermaid. "Tell us how you were wild."

"I once drank a bottle of whiskey and stayed up all night playing an online poker tournament. Where I had to bet real money."

The women all made dutifully impressed noises. "Very wild," Jolie said.

"Okay, fine. Hmmm… how about this? I ziplined naked. There! That's wild, right?"

At the silence in the car, Ted looked around.

"What? Is that not wild? I thought it was. Especially when I realized I had nothing to protect my…self if I fell or crashed."

"Erm… we're pretty free with nudity around here." Mirra reached back and patted Ted on the arm. "But the ziplining adds another element. You get points for that."

"Points! That's it? Tough crowd," Ted said and shook his head sorrowfully.

"Was there a crowd of people waiting in line? That would add more points," Jolie offered.

"No," Ted said with a sigh. "It was a private house in the jungle."

"Well, in the jungle is tough. There could have been a very dangerous spider that might have taken a bite of your nether regions. You could have died! Very wild, Ted," Irma supplied as they pulled off by a line of cars leading to a thatched villa set atop a cliff.

"As a matter of fact, there were many dangerous things and I very well *could* have died. So I'll take my macho points, thank you very much," Ted said.

Jolie bit her lip to keep from laughing. "Come on, wild thing, let's go get drunk and dance naked around the fire," she said, gesturing to the people streaming to the villa.

Music pulsed from the wide deck that wrapped around the front of the villa and the sound of voices and laughter floated to them. The sun, hanging just at the horizon, shot brilliant pink streaks across the water.

"Um, just *how* comfortable are you all with nudity?"

Ted asked, the faint pink on his cheeks again, and the women all laughed.

"Don't worry, Theodore. We haven't brought you to a nudist colony."

"Yet…" Ted muttered under his breath.

Jolie laughed again. She couldn't remember the last time she'd laughed this much, let alone snorted with laughter. "That's on the agenda for next week," she promised.

"I'll be sure to stay out of cold water then," Ted promised, and Irma interrupted their banter by beckoning Ted to follow with the cooler and the hamper.

"I like him," Mirra whispered to Jolie, following behind the two. "He's just so… great."

"Isn't he?"

"Striptease. Go slow. Let him do his thing tonight, but just kind of stay within sight. You want him watching you when you can catch his eye. Red was a good color choice for that."

"I think I'm starting to want him to like me for more than my looks," Jolie said, mulling over how much she enjoyed talking with Ted. The fact that he made her laugh so readily was worth everything in her book. But could she engage his mind as well?

"Oh, this is music to my ears." Mirra all but bounced in her sandals. "I love this for you, Jolie. Finally you want someone who will see you for you and all you have to offer."

"You act like my past lovers didn't see that in me."

"They saw what you allowed them to see. Which is fine, because it was sex and we, as women, have every right to enjoy and be confident in our sexuality. But you already know this one is different. The oracle *told* you so. And I for one am so here for it."

"Well, tonight I just striptease, remember?"

"Excuse me? Is there actually going to be nudity tonight?" Ted's expression danced between hope and embarrassment, and Mirra let out a peal of laughter as she hooked his arm and dragged him away from a gaping Jolie.

"No, we were talking about something else. Get us a drink, Jolie," Mirra called over her shoulder.

Jolie went inside the villa to help Irma stash the cooler and put out their food. The main room of the villa was one wide-open space, with a kitchen area in one corner and the rest of the room open to the long line of screened windows and doors that opened to the huge wrap-around deck where people were gathering to watch the sunset. They'd already started the bonfire and a few people swayed to music from an iPod while some of the local musicians set up their equipment in the corner of the deck. Jolie knew most people here and she didn't get far into the party without stopping to greet people she knew.

Jolie delivered ice-cold beers to Ted and Mirra, then, taking her sister's advice, she moved away to mingle. Time passed quickly as she moved from group to group, catching up on the local gossip – or as they liked to call it, the coconut telegraph. Finally, she circled back around to where Ted sat with Prince and a few of his fisherman buddies. Sitting on the arm of Prince's chair, Jolie crossed her legs and leaned in.

It pleased her when Ted paused and did a double take

at her legs before offering her a smile and continuing his conversation.

"Jared's telling him 'bout de time he seen a mermaid." Prince motioned to a fisherman buddy of his who was gesticulating wildly with his hands as he told his story.

"And Ted's eating it up?"

"Oh, he's lovin' it. It's nice, you know? Most of dese guys don't get to tell dese stories and have people actually believe 'em."

"I'd say he's working up to believing."

"Dat's not all dat bad either, Jolie."

"It was nice of you to invite him. Your parties are legendary."

"Bet he thought he was going to some little beach party." Prince chuckled and held up his empty bottle when Maria waved at him from across the room.

"He actually had a good read on you, Prince. He said he thought you probably had your hands in many businesses in town."

"I told you I liked him."

"I do too."

"Music's getting hot. Dance with de man."

"Only if you dance with me first," Jolie said.

"Me? Oh, I'll dance you off your feet, Miss Thang," Prince drawled and hopped up. Ted glanced up as everyone began to stand.

"Everyone is loosening up now. We're going to dance," Jolie told him.

"Oh, okay. I'll just watch from here…" Ted trailed off as Maria materialized at his side and handed him a large glass. She gave another one to Jolie, and a beer to Prince.

"You're my queen," Prince said. "Is dere anything I can do to help you, my love?"

"You dance with this pretty girl. Then you dance with me after. You'll see who's better," Maria promised, shooting Jolie a wink from her twinkling brown eyes.

"You don't deserve that woman," Jolie decided as they made their way to the sand. She took a sip of her drink and raised her eyebrow at the liberal amount of rum in the punch. Prince was famous for his rum punch. She'd have to keep an eye on Ted.

"Don't I know it. I do my best to keep her happy."

"What's your secret?" Jolie asked, bending to untie her strappy sandals and toss them to the side. Glancing over her shoulder as she stood up, she caught a shell-shocked look on Ted's face and realized she'd just bent over in front of him in her very short dress. Whoops, Jolie thought, and then sent him a saucy little smile.

"Surrender, Miss Jolie. Surrender."

"Surrender is your secret?" Jolie asked, as Prince wrapped an arm around her and bounced into step with her.

"Sure is. You see, at de end of de day, dat woman has never asked me for anything dat's worth a fight. She loves me and she looks out for me. I don't care if she want to paint de walls blue or buy more cushions for de couch. Or if she want me to eat more greens and go for walks. She keeps me happy and dat's what matters. Why fight it? Surrender is really de answer."

"Interesting. But don't you feel like you lose yourself?"

"No, I don't. She respects me, you see? She listens to

my opinions. I'm not a doormat. I just don't bother getting
fussed about things dat don't matter all dat much."

"You're a smart man."

"So's Ted. I think I've got enough rum in him you can
lure him out for a dance." With that, Prince twirled her
toward Ted, and she landed – half-laughing, half-gasping –
in front of him as he stood at the edge of the circle
watching the dancers.

"Your turn," Jolie declared.

"Oh… I –"

"Come on, wild man, live a little," Jolie teased.

Ted put down his drink. He wrapped his arm around
her waist, then paused, and she realized he was counting
the beats before he swung her into the circle moving
around the fire.

Well, now, wasn't this interesting, Jolie thought as Ted
moved with her in time to the beat of the music. Not only
did the man have rhythm, but he knew how to move.
Closing her eyes for a moment, she just allowed herself to
be led to the song, enjoying the feel of his arms around
her, and the pulse of energy that thickened between them
to its own more primitive beat. When she opened her eyes,
Jolie caught Ted looking down at her, the fire reflected in
his eyes. If this was any other man and any other moment,
Jolie would have leaned up and kissed him.

Instead, she reached up and patted his cheek.

"You've got moves, Dr. Macalister. I'm impressed."

"Jolie…" Ted trailed off and gulped.

"I think your next dance partner has arrived. You can't
say no to Maria," Jolie said, backing away so the short
round woman at their side could take her place. Turning,

she blew out a breath and headed for the bar. She needed a cold drink. Now.

Mirra caught her eye as she walked past and gave her a thumbs-up.

Rum was the answer, she decided.

CHAPTER 21

*J*olie was too antsy to sleep when they returned home, so she decided to make her way down to the beach. They'd laughingly nudged a very cheerful and decidedly tipsy Ted up to his room. He really was adorable, Jolie thought as she tightened the tie of the silky robe she'd slipped on. It was a good thing he wasn't an angry drunk; she wasn't sure how she would've handled that. It was nice to know that Ted only became more cheerful with drink.

She'd wanted to go upstairs with him.

Not to even have sex or anything like that – he was so incredibly charming that Jolie would have enjoyed just cuddling up and laughing with him. There was something adorably rumpled about a tipsy Ted that made Jolie want to take care of him.

Now the water called to her. When she couldn't sleep at night, she always took to the water. Nothing cleared her head more than slipping into the darkness and allowing the cool water to soothe her angsty soul. Jolie reached for her waist to untie the belt of her robe when she heard movement behind her.

"Jolie."

Jolie closed her eyes for a moment, a smile hovering on her lips, then turned to look at Ted standing behind her. He wore no shirt, just loose drawstring shorts, and she saw for the first time just how in shape he was. She wanted to trace the dip and curve of each of his muscles with her finger… and then follow with her mouth. Instead, she smiled at him in confusion.

"I thought we put you to bed, Ted."

"Oh no. Was I being that annoying? I'm sorry," Ted said, hanging his head and digging his toe into the sand.

"I don't think it's possible for you to be annoying," Jolie said with a laugh.

"Tell that to my sister."

"Well, that's a different story. I just meant I was surprised to see you out here. Are you planning to go for a swim? I might caution you against that since you've been drinking."

"No, no swimming in dark water for me. That's for sure. Did you know there are sharks in there? They hunt at night, don't they? That's probably a bad combination – me flailing around next to a hungry shark. No thank you, I'll pass."

"Just for the record, the ocean is the shark's home. And truly, they don't single out humans as some sort of tasty treat to snack on."

"That's true. And I won't lie, I'm obsessed with Shark Week. I just don't trust myself to remain calm if one decided to come have a lick."

"A *lick?*" Jolie's voice went up an octave and she slapped a hand over her mouth to stop a snort from popping out. "Sharks do not lick."

"Well, a taste then. A sampling. You know, like when a dog comes up and licks you, then bites you."

"When has that ever happened to you?" Jolie demanded.

"What? A dog licking and then biting me? Um, probably never. Most definitely not. That sounds more like a cat thing, doesn't it? Like when they roll over on their back and look all cuddly, like they want pets, and you go on in and they maul your hand."

"Right, got it. Sharks that lick and cats that maul. Is that what brought you down here?" They'd begun to stroll the beach, and had quickly fallen into step with each other. The waves were gentle on the sand and the moon bright enough to light their way. It felt companionable and right, strolling in the darkness with him like that.

"No. I saw you from the balcony. It looked like you might go in the water. I was worried about you."

"Were you? You've had more to drink than me." Jolie tilted her head to look up at him.

"Nevertheless, I wouldn't be able to settle in if I knew you were out here letting sharks lick you."

"You have a twisted mind, Dr. Macalister."

"Also… there's something…"

Jolie stopped to look at Ted, sensing the very real frustration in his voice. He ran a hand through his hair, looked up to the sky, then back down to where she stood in her silky slip of a robe. Her heart pounded when his eyes met hers and held.

"Listen, I don't know how to explain this."

"Okay…" Jolie drew out the word. "Why don't you try?"

"I have something for you."

"For me? A gift?" Warmth rushed through Jolie.

"Yes. No. Yes."

"Hmmm." Jolie studied Ted while he clearly struggled with a decision.

"Yes. But I can't explain why. Apparently, I'm supposed to give this to someone. And the only person I can think of is you. And when I saw you standing out by the water, I realized – it's you."

"It's me?" Jolie asked, her voice hopeful.

"Yes, this should go to you. In fact, I may be wrong, but I think it's yours anyway. This belongs to you." Ted dug in his pocket and pulled something out, holding his hand up to the light.

Jolie gasped at the necklace entwined in his fingers. The pendant mirrored the design on her comb.

Her hand reached up, then paused in the air. She wanted this necklace so badly, but wasn't sure if he fully understood what he was doing. It didn't seem fair to accept until he knew the meaning of his gesture. "It's lovely, Ted."

"I'm supposed to give this to you. I'm sure of it," Ted said.

"You might be. But I'm not sure you understand why."

"I don't think I've understood a lot of the undercurrents I've noticed since I set foot on this island."

Jolie angled her head to meet his eyes. So, he did feel more than he was letting on…

"Where did you find this necklace, Ted?" Jolie asked, turning to start walking again. Ted fell in step next to her, threading the necklace between his hands.

After a pause, he said, "Well, shit. You're going to think I'm crazy."

"Do you really think that?"

"Actually, no; you're probably the only one who would believe me. What with your proclivity for magick and all."

"Ah." Jolie smiled. She walked just inside the tide line, where the sand was packed tight and the water tickled her toes. Her body itched to dive into the sea, to feel the water cocoon her, but that could wait.

"Sorry, now I'm implying you're crazy for believing in magick. I'm fumbling this."

"Just tell me what happened, and I'll reserve judgment."

Ted recounted his dream; Jolie closed her eyes, surprised the oracle had visited him so directly.

"And then, when I woke up, this necklace was in my hands. It went from my dream to my hands. In real life. Like it was just… there."

"That is fascinating. And it most certainly is magick. Are you a believer yet?"

"I… I don't have any other explanation. I've been obsessing over it and aside from one of you slipping into my room and leaving it in my bed…" Ted let the words hang.

"I can assure you none of us would go into your room without your permission. Although if you invited me…" Jolie let that hang as well. He was tipsy, so she was taking a risk on whether he would remember her boldness, but she wanted to test the waters.

"So, magick then. That's it? That's the answer?" Ted asked, looking down in frustration at the necklace – and completely skipping past her hint.

"That's it, Ted. I told you – Siren Island has its secrets, and magick is real."

"Why you? Is this your necklace?" Ted turned to her and held it out in the moonlight again. Her heart leapt. Yes, she wanted to scream – yes, this is my necklace, but only because you choose to give it to me.

"The necklace belongs to whomever you give it to."

"The goddess said I would know who it belongs to. And I know it's yours. So… here." Ted offered it again and Jolie laughed. Reaching out, she touched his forearm, pushing the necklace back from her a bit.

"Before I accept, would you like to learn a little more about mermaid society?"

"Always," Ted said.

They resumed their walk, the moonlight bathing their path, the ocean providing their background music.

"Mermaids often mate for life," Jolie began. "It isn't expected. And having one partner isn't necessarily the norm. Some mermaids choose multiple partners and form a unit; they're all happily in a relationship together. Others choose monogamy, and still others are content to have a variety of lovers throughout their lives without ever really committing. Each choice is accepted in mermaid culture, and sexuality is… loose, should I say? Nobody frowns on what would be considered 'promiscuous' here; nobody blinks an eye at men choosing men as partners, or women choosing women. Mermaid society assumes that each individual will make the choice that's most beneficial for a happy and healthy life."

"That's very forward-thinking," Ted observed.

"It is. But also, because the society isn't that large, there's no use policing such matters and risking alienating your own people – do you understand?"

"I do."

"However, for those who choose to be monogamous, there's a ceremony that will bond them for life. And with that ceremony come certain adornments."

"Adornments…" Ted stopped and looked at her, then down at the necklace he held.

"That's correct. What you have there is a ceremonial bonding necklace. In human culture, this would be the equivalent of an engagement ring."

"I… wait… so I…"

"Yes. In the mermaid world, your giving me that necklace would mean you were proposing a lifetime union together. Or proposing marriage, however you'd like to look at it." Jolie held her breath as she looked up at him, her heart pounding in her chest.

"Oh. Oh my. I… well… I certainly didn't mean that. I was just convinced I'd found something that belonged to you. I didn't mean for it to… Oh, I'm sorry, Jolie. I hope I didn't offend you by offering this. Thank you for the explanation."

Jolie's stomach flipped and she turned away, fighting down the tears that threatened. Why did she want to cry? He hadn't known what he was offering.

"That's fine. But I think you'll want to keep that and

spend some time with it. You'll know when you find the right person to give it to."

"But I was certain it was for you…" Ted looked down at her.

"Well, maybe that was the alcohol speaking," Jolie said, to give him an out. Then she turned and patted him on the arm. "Why don't you head back up? I'm going to raid the kitchen for more brownies."

She turned and hightailed it back to the villa, knowing he would follow her. All she wanted to do was swim until the ocean took her tears away, but she knew Ted would never go inside if he thought she was about to go for a night swim.

"Thank you for the explanation. You've given me a lot to mull over," Ted said when they reached the villa. "Sleep well, Jolie. I'm sorry if I overstepped any boundaries this evening."

"You haven't. Sweet dreams, Dr. Macalister," Jolie said, and shut the kitchen door before leaning back against it and blowing out a breath.

There wasn't enough chocolate in the world to take away this ache, she realized, rubbing her hand over her chest.

But it was worth a try.

CHAPTER 22

*H*e dreamed of Jolie.

Every night now, he dreamed of her. He'd taken to having more than one glass of wine at night to try and lull himself into a dreamless sleep, but nothing seemed to help. Every night, like clockwork, she showed up in his dreams.

It made him want to pull his hair out, Ted thought, sketching in his journal as he treated himself to a rare cigar on his balcony. Even the shape taking form under his pen was Jolie's face, the curves of her body, the flip of her tail fin, the…

Her tail fin?

He threw his pencil down at that and leaned back to look at the night sky. Rubbing a palm over his face, he took a lingering drag of his cigar and a sip of the whisky he'd chosen to pair with it. The full moon was near, he realized; the pretty orb shone down on the dark water below him.

At first he'd been slightly embarrassed about his ignorance when he'd tried to give Jolie the necklace the other night. But he hadn't known that was a tradition with mermaids, nor was Jolie a mermaid, so he'd finally talked himself out of his embarrassment and gone down to breakfast the next day. She'd greeted him with a breezy hello and hadn't acted any different, so he pushed the embarrassment aside and moved on. Though he had put some distance between them. Not because he didn't want her getting thoughts about him or developing a crush, but because these ridiculous dreams were hounding him and making him think some decidedly unprofessional thoughts about his colleague.

Who was also Irma's daughter, he reminded himself, and Irma was someone he definitely did not want to anger.

At first, he'd chalked the dreams up to the normal lustful dreams that can happen when a man's in the company of beautiful women. Jolie was, quite simply put, the most stunning woman he'd ever laid eyes on. It stood to reason that his brain would pick up on that and put her in many a naughty position in his dreams.

And oh, were they naughty.

Ted groaned again; his body ached for release. In his dreams he gave himself permission to savor every inch of her luscious body. Which he did, over and over again, until he woke, his body raging with lust for her. But after he'd given in to sating his need for her, the other dreams appeared.

Dreams where they walked together, laughing. Flashes of her surprise when she snorted with laughter, or him admiring how her face lit up when she talked about something that interested her. The in-between moments when he watched Jolie, hoping she didn't see him looking. It was like electricity crackled around her – and as the days wore on, Ted was beginning to think he'd be willing to be shocked.

Except, of course, that a woman like Jolie would never, ever, look twice at a man like Ted.

"Shit, it's hard to get rid of those thoughts," Ted said out loud, and took another puff of his cigar. His therapist had reminded him over and over that negative self-talk was keeping him from finding a partner. He'd gotten better at talking himself up as the years went by. He'd grown more confident in who he was as a person and the direction he was taking with his life. But when it came to women – especially women who were the total package, like Jolie – he was transported right back to being the nerdy kid that all the other kids laughed at. It had taken him weeks to work up the courage to finally ask a shy girl in his class to a school dance one year. That had been his mistake, Ted mused, tapping the cigar gently on an ashtray. He should have asked her somewhere privately. For a moment, he had thought she'd say yes – until the other girls, having overheard, started laughing and making fun of her. She'd run crying from the room and had never spoken to Ted after.

It had taken him a long time to get over that.

You're an accomplished adult, Theodore. You have a lot to offer a partner. You'll never cheat, you can provide financially, and you can offer good conversation. Ted repeated his little mantras to himself and felt the tight band across his chest lessen a little.

He'd even managed to have a few long-term relationships, for which he was incredibly grateful. He was still friendly with his exes; they had all parted amicably, and one had even begun trying to set him up with other women. Ted had introduced her to his best friend, who had since become her husband. Some might think it was weird, but he was just happy for them. Life was too short to be jealous or hold grudges.

Ted's gaze dropped back to the journal where he'd been sketching Jolie as a mermaid. The other dreams had started after the lustful ones. These were more fantastical, featuring Jolie as a gorgeous mermaid; together they'd swim deep into the ocean. Though how that didn't send panic through him, Ted did not know. While he was a strong swimmer, dark water was just not his thing. Yet here he was, frolicking in his dreams with Jolie in the dark water night after night.

This island was getting to him.

Maybe that was it. Perhaps just talking to people incessantly about mermaids was seeping into his dreams. And because Jolie was so beautiful, of course she was taking on the role of mermaid in his dreams. It wasn't a far jump, and was the only one he felt comfortable with. The other conclusion... well, that was just absurd.

His eyes trailed to the necklace, which he'd placed on a hook by his bed. It hung there like a glowing piece of wall art, and if Ted didn't know better he would have said the piece called to him. Every single time he walked past it, he could feel the tug of the stones.

And he knew, in his heart of hearts, that this necklace was meant for Jolie.

"I must be going mad."

CHAPTER 23

"*W*here are you off to today?"

"I'm taking him to Nalachi's reef," Jolie said, examining the contents of the cooler she'd put on the kitchen counter.

"Really?" Irma looked up from typing on her MacBook. Mirra had left to the shops for the morning, so it was just the two of them sharing a breakfast.

"Really."

"That's interesting. Pay my respects, please," Irma said, and Jolie held up a small hemp bag she'd put to the side.

"I have some hibiscus and coriander in here. I'll spread it while we're in the water."

"Herbs for love, I see."

"Isn't that what paying respects is? Giving love?" Jolie snapped, then reached up to pinch the bridge of her nose. "I'm sorry. I didn't sleep well."

"Again? Are you having bad dreams?"

"No. Dreaming would mean I'm sleeping, Mother."

Jolie shot her a look and Irma held up her hands in the universal 'Don't hurt me, I'm just trying to help' signal.

"Ugh, sorry again."

"Why don't I make you a nice espresso. It'll perk you right up."

"I won't say no." Jolie went to the fridge and pulled out some fruit and a wedge of cheese to add to the cooler. She also added a baguette, two bottles of wine, double the amount of water, and a container of Irma's oatmeal chocolate chip cookies. That should set them up for the day.

"Jolie, why don't you just tell him how you feel?"

"Um, because I can't. That's why."

"Sure you can."

"No, I really can't. He has to choose me. The oracle showed it in her reading."

"But he can still choose you after you tell him your feelings. I'm certain there are no rules about that."

"I just... I want him to pick me. I want him to see me and love me for me."

"Then keep showing him who you are. I don't know anyone who wouldn't fall in love with you. You're amazing."

Jolie turned and hugged her mother, sighing into her arms.

"Of course, that's because you're my daughter and all."

"Glad to hear your ego hasn't diminished with time." Jolie laughed and poked her in the ribs.

"You say ego, I say confidence."

"Thank you for the espresso." Jolie took the little cup Irma offered and downed it like a shot, then stood at the counter and checked to make sure she had everything she needed for the day.

"How about this?"

"What?" Jolie turned and looked at Irma.

"Take today without any expectation on you. Forget what the oracle said. Forget being magickal. Forget any sort of pressure. Just go have fun."

"Just like that?"

"Sure, why not? It's only one day. You can go back to obsessing over your future tomorrow. But, for today, relax. I know you hate being out of control, but you can't control love or love's timing. So if you can't control it – let it be. You're only going to stress yourself out more, which is likely why you aren't sleeping much."

"So, go with the flow."

"Yes, my little mermaid. Allow your troubles to float away with the tides. They'll wash back in when you're ready to deal with them again."

"Okay, that's not bad advice." Jolie took a deep breath, then another, rolling her head on her neck and allowing the tension to ease from her. "You're right. Nothing has to be decided today."

"You've always been my more stubborn child," Irma mused, "kicking butt through life and leveling anyone who stands in your way. I can imagine this has you feeling out of sorts."

"I do feel a bit rudderless, yes," Jolie admitted.

"Just remember that when the future is undecided, anything is achievable."

"How so?"

"Don't you see? Right now, you're uncomfortable

because you aren't in control. You don't know what the future holds, so it's making you angsty. You're assuming the worst – that nothing will go your way, that it'll all fail. But the opposite could be true as well. Everything could be amazing. So if you're going to give this much weight to the potential negative outcomes, then it's only fair that you give the positive outcomes a turn on the dancefloor too."

"Have I mentioned you can be annoying?"

"Only every day. I love you, Jolie. My stubborn, strong-willed, beautiful girl. I'm so proud of the woman you've become."

"Oh, great, now you're making me weepy." Jolie brushed a tear away with the back of her hand. "I love you too. I couldn't have asked for a better mother than you."

"There isn't one. Because I am meant for you and you are meant for me. And so our fates intertwine. Now, I think I hear Ted on the stairs."

"I feel better. I'm going to swim and relax and enjoy the day," Jolie decided. "Like a mini-vacation."

"From what? This tough job you have?"

"Oh please. I don't see *you* cleaning the guest rooms," Jolie groused as she hefted the cooler from the counter.

"That's because I pulled rank."

"I'll bring it up at our quarterly meeting."

"I look forward to it."

It was hard to say who had more points in their battle of wills, but Jolie thought she and Irma were pretty even.

Humming a tune under her breath, she walked out into the sunshine to greet Ted. He'd been busy as of late and they'd spent less time together, so today would be a nice treat. She'd suggested they go visit

Nalachi's Reef, which required renting a boat, and they could explore the area from the water. Ted had brightened when she'd suggested it, so today should be a fun day.

He looked good, Jolie thought with a sigh, as he immediately rushed over to help her with the cooler. The sun had finally gotten to him, and he sported a golden tan which only highlighted the green of his eyes. He looked relaxed today, in loose blue swim shorts and a Billabong tank top. Jolie was fairly certain he hadn't had those clothes when he'd arrived.

"Have you been shopping? You look like you're going surfing."

"Not good? I hit up a store downtown where a very pushy woman decided exactly what I was going to wear, and even made me try it on and model it for the entire store."

"Ah, yes. Miss Maureen?"

"That's the one."

"She's a force of nature. But she knows what she's talking about. And you look really good, so she steered you in the right direction."

"I'm not sure she steered so much as shoved, but I like the look." Ted looked down at his clothes. "And it's nice and breathable."

"Good. It'll be hot on the water, so you'll want extra sunscreen."

"Already applied – and I brought a rash guard too."

"Smart. Shall we?"

"We shall." Ted held the door open for her as he always did, then rounded the front of the truck. Soon they were headed toward the marina, the windows open and the music playing a soft kicky island tune on low.

"I haven't seen much of you the last couple days. Have you been working on your paper?" Jolie asked, digging in her tote for her sunglasses.

"Yes, I have been. Well, compiling notes really. I... oh gosh, this sounds silly. Never mind." Ted shook his head, a smile hovering on his lips.

"Um, you know you can't just drop that and then not say anything else. I'm entirely too curious to let that go."

"Okay, since you're my research assistant and all, I suppose I can tell you under professional confidentiality."

"Are you asking me to keep a secret?" Jolie pushed away the feeling that was rising in her at being referred to as just 'his assistant.' At this point, she was hoping for 'friend' at the very least. "Even if I didn't work for you, I'm still your friend. I can keep a secret."

"I'm sorry; I shouldn't assume that you can't keep a secret. I'm just nervous about it, is all. And you're right – you are a friend."

"And..."

"Well, the more time I've spent listening to everyone's stories and learning about the legends here, the less certain I am how it would all fit into a paper. There are so many interesting tales. So honestly, I think... well, I think I'm going to write a book."

"Are you?" Jolie punched his arm. "That's amazing, Ted! Have you ever considered writing a book before?"

"I mean, it's certainly crossed my mind. I'm a litera-ture professor, after all. I think everyone in my entire department has dreamed about writing a book at some point in our lives. There's a saying though: Those who can't do, teach."

"Really?" Jolie laughed. "I've never heard that before."

"I don't think it holds a ton of truth, but there is something to it. Either way, I think I'm going to give it a real try."

"Will you write it as fiction?"

"I'm toying with both angles. But I'm leaning toward non-fiction – well, as non-fiction as it can be, writing about mermaids. I think, however, it would be quite intriguing to relate all the mermaid encounters as told by locals, and let the reader decide what they believe instead of trying to force anything on them."

"That's very noble of you. Frankly, you've been very open-minded with everyone you've spoken to, for being a nonbeliever yourself."

"It's not that I'm a *non*believer." Ted sighed and tapped his fingers on the steering wheel as they turned into the marina parking lot.

"But you're not yet a full believer."

"To quote a great American artist, I'm halfway there."

"Oh jeez." Jolie laughed and shook her head as they got out of the truck. "Fine. I like the idea of letting the reader decide. Do you have a title?"

"I'm thinking of *Close Encounters of the Mermaid Kind*."

Jolie paused and looked at him across the bed of the pickup truck where they were grabbing their supplies.

"You most certainly are not."

"I'm most certainly not. But I kind of like it."

"What about *Mermaid Moments: The Magick of Siren Island?*"

"Wait." Ted dropped the cooler and pulled his phone from his pocket. "Let me write that down before I forget it. I like it."

"I get half the royalties."

"You drive a hard bargain, Jolie."

"I'm open to negotiation."

"No royalties but I'll buy you dinner?"

"No deal. Five percent and you can buy me a dog."

"A dog?" Ted paused at the gate to the marina. "You want a dog?"

"I've always wanted a dog. But it's best not to have one at the guesthouse; people have allergies and stuff. We have our next-door neighbor dog friend, Pipin, so I get enough cuddle time."

"You should have your own dog," Ted insisted.

"Why? I get enough dog time, it's fine."

"Because you deserve everything you want."

"Finally, someone who recognizes my greatness. Bow before me," Jolie joked, breaking the moment, and Ted finally laughed. It was odd, the way he'd looked at her, but she decided to file that away for later. Today was a no-pressure day and she promised herself to keep it that way.

"I may not bow, but I will carry your parcels, milady." Ted gestured to where their boat was docked. "The queen may go first."

"Yes! This is how I deserve to be treated." Jolie strolled toward a man standing at the end of the dock, saying, "Come along then, peasant. Place my stuff in the boat."

"Hello?" the man said, looking from Jolie to Ted and back.

"I'm queen for the day. He decided it. Not me." Jolie smiled broadly at the man, who immediately smiled back.

"In that case, may I help you aboard, my queen?" The man performed a sweeping bow, and then held out his hand to her. He helped her down to the boat while Ted dropped their belongings in the stern.

"Thank you, good sir." Jolie smiled and kissed the man's cheek.

"Oh, sure. I do all the hard work and he gets the kiss," Ted griped.

Jolie laughed, absolutely delighted with him, and leaned over to peck a smacking kiss to his cheek. She ignored the rush of heat that flowed through her when her lips touched his skin.

Keep it light, Jolie, keep it light.

"You've both served me well this fine day. You may rest now." Jolie waved them away and let Ted get all the instructions from the man while she settled into her seat. She could drive a boat as easily as she could swim, and knew the reefs and danger spots around the island like the back of her hand. There was nobody safer for him to be on this charter with.

"All ready, my queen?" Ted asked, moving to stand by the wheel.

"I was born ready."

CHAPTER 24

"Well, it turns out that I can't actually chauffeur the queen," Ted admitted, having been relegated to the passenger seat of the boat about five minutes into the ride after he'd almost side-swiped two docked yachts and corrected his course so violently that he nearly took out the dock on the opposite side of the marina.

Jolie was still laughing. Kneeling on the captain's chair, she easily navigated the boat through the marina and out into the open water, steering into the darker blue of the deeper water so she wouldn't have to concentrate so much on watching for any snorkelers or kayakers.

"You were so confident!" Jolie kept laughing. It was the first time she'd really seen Ted flustered, and she had enjoyed every minute.

"What did that man call me?"

"Um… best not to repeat it in public."

"Rude. Can't he see I'm a beginner?" Ted huffed and crossed his arms.

"He saw. We all could. Any idea how much it costs to fix a hole in a yacht hull?"

"Probably my yearly salary," Ted mumbled.

"We are a fairly friendly population here, but, you know – some things may upset us more than others."

"He probably wasn't from here anyway."

"Right, that's it." Jolie smirked as they rode around the point of the island, coming along the west coast where the winds were calmer. As the sun baked down on her, she stood and shimmied out of her jean shorts and tank, bending to fold them and put them in her tote. Pulling out a sarong, Jolie draped it over the warm leather of the captain's chair and settled in to give Ted a tour of the island from the water.

"So, coming up is the water view of the beach we went to the other..." Jolie trailed off as she saw Ted standing as if frozen, staring at her. She looked down to make sure a breast hadn't fallen out of her top or something. Nope, everything seemed to be tucked into place. "Is everything okay?"

"Ah, sorry, my brain just froze for a second. Ever have that happen? Haha... you know... just, mind kind of drifts away..." Ted made a fluttery motion with his hand and clamped his lips shut, turning away.

"Sure, I have those moments. It happens to the best of us."

"The beach?" Ted said, his tone a little harsh. Jolie raised an eyebrow at his turned head. If she didn't know better, she'd say he had been checking her out in her bikini. So what if she had picked a particularly skimpy suit to wear that day? Most of her suits were skimpy; it was as close to swimming naked as she was allowed in public.

"Um, yes, the beach. See? That's where we were the other day." Jolie pulled the throttle back and slowed the boat. "With the cave that had the etching."

"Fascinating. It looks totally different from the water. Wow, if I hadn't been there already, I'd say it was impossible to get to by foot." Ted took out his phone and took a series of shots as Jolie maneuvered the boat a bit closer.

"Remember the ledge we walked across? The tide is higher now, so the water would likely be up to your knees."

"It truly looks like a hidden paradise."

"The mermaids chose wisely for their art space," Jolie said, cutting the engine completely and letting them float for a bit. Waves slapped the hull of the boat lightly, and they rocked gently with the motion of the water while Ted studied the beach.

"Do you think…" Ted began, then shrugged. "Never mind."

"Go ahead," Jolie said.

"I recall you mentioning we could camp there one night. A full moon's coming up – can we camp there then? Or – well, I guess that's outside your job description. Can I go camp there? Would it be safe? Or would I be violating island laws or anything?"

"Siren Island isn't that strict when it comes to camping, so no, you wouldn't be breaking any laws. And I don't mind going camping with you. Despite how it may seem, I'm a nature girl at heart."

"Are you?" Ted glanced back, his gaze skimming over

her quickly before darting away. "Have you taken any camping trips before?"

"Just on-island here. I quite enjoy sleeping under the stars. You just need a hammock and you can rock yourself all night long."

"Have you ever hiked in the mountains?" Ted asked as Jolie started the boat and continued down the coastline.

"No, I've never been off-island." Jolie waited for the response that typically followed.

"You haven't? Is that by choice or because of life circumstances?" It was probably the nicest way anyone had ever responded to that comment, Jolie mused; most people were shocked, or thought her ignorant to be so poorly traveled. Not everyone considered that it could be a financial situation, which she assumed was what Ted was thinking. In reality, she couldn't leave. Mermaids had a lot of magick, but flying in a plane was not something they could do. If she wanted to travel, it was in her mermaid form, and for that she was restricted to neighboring islands.

"Life circumstances."

"I'm sorry; I shouldn't assume that everyone is able to travel," Ted said, immediately contrite.

"No worries, Ted. For someone who isn't able to travel, I certainly live in a gorgeous spot, don't I?"

"It's hard to argue with that," Ted said, turning to take in the rolling green hills of the island and the turquoise water that surrounded it. "I don't think I'd be too bothered about not leaving here."

"Really? Wouldn't you miss snow? I hear it's like confetti falling from the sky."

"You've never seen snow?" Ted exclaimed.

Jolie laughed, gesturing around her. "Where would I see snow?"

"Of course; you're right. Listen, I've had enough snow in my life to enjoy never having to deal with it again. Sure, it's charming when it first falls to the ground and you can curl up with a blanket, a fire, and a good book – but by the time a nor'easter hits, well, I'm over it."

"What's a nor'easter? It sounds like a monster."

"It can be. It's kind of like a hurricane. But with snow."

"Ouch."

"Ouch indeed. And afterward, when you're shoveling your car out of three feet of snow and your face has frozen and it hurts to breathe the air –" Ted put his hand out to the ocean. "This is all you can dream about."

"Hmm. I think I'd just like to see a light sprinkling of snow then. Not a snow hurricane."

"Yes, a light dusting is ideal for charming moments."

"I think I've just always seen those snowy Christmas moments with a dog frolicking across the yard and being able to see your breath. It seems like another world. Just once, I'd like to see it."

"Maybe we can get you up to Boston sometime in the winter. I could business expense a flight for you, if that makes it easier."

It wouldn't, but Jolie appreciated the offer. It made her realize that despite Ted's wish to keep her at a professional distance, he did consider her a friend, at the very least.

"Oh! There's the statue! Look how magnificent from the water! It looks even more amazing than on land. Oh…

just look at her. She's holding herself so proudly over the water. And yet, there's a sadness to her, isn't there? Or is it fierceness? Maybe both…" Ted was standing and taking photos, and Jolie studied the mermaid statue high on the cliffs.

"She's all of those things. Sad for love lost. Fierce about protecting her reefs and her island. Beautiful for being powerful."

"Yes, exactly that. You'll have to repeat that for my book. Maybe you could write the foreword? You have a lovely way with words," Ted said over his shoulder. He continued to take photos of the statue, unaware that his words had left Jolie stunned, her mouth hanging open in awe.

He wanted her to write a chapter in his book? He liked her words? Nobody, aside from her family or a select few friends, had ever seen her for her mind before. It was always her looks that received the first compliments. And this man – a Harvard professor, no less – not only thought she had a beautiful way with words, but would trust her to write for his book? Tears pricked her eyes and she had to look away from him and down to the water for a moment, pulling on the ocean's calming energy to soothe the emotions that threatened to boil over.

If she had any doubts about her feelings for him before, they were all washed away.

"Are you okay?" Ted asked, and she realized he'd left his seat to stand by her side. Reaching out, he touched her arm, trying to catch a look at her face, which she'd turned away from him. Jolie was going to brush it off, but remembering Mirra's words about being vulnerable, she chose the more courageous path.

"I'm really touched you would consider me for writing something in your book. Nobody... well, nobody's ever treated me like that before."

"Like what, Jolie?" Ted said, now stroking her arm. She wondered if he even realized he was doing it.

"Like I have brains. That I'm not just all..." Jolie gestured to her body. "That I have something interesting to say or contribute to this world."

"Ah," Ted said, belatedly realizing he was touching her and pulling his hand back. "I see."

"It's just really nice of you to ask me. I guess I hadn't realized how meaningful something like that would be. It makes me feel respected for something other than my looks."

"Well, first of all, I wouldn't have asked if I didn't mean it. I don't make frivolous comments and I don't play games. So the invitation was sincere, and I do admire your way with words and storytelling."

"Oh, you're going to get me going again." Jolie laughed and dabbed at her eyes behind her sunglasses. She cut the motor and let the boat rock in the waves for a moment.

"May I offer you an objective view?"

"You may." Jolie smiled a watery smile at Ted. Of course he would ask her so politely, instead of just subjecting her to his thoughts.

"You're gorgeous. In fact, I think you're the most beautiful woman I've ever seen."

Jolie's heart flipped inside her at his words. But she'd

heard it before, so she wasn't completely blown away by his comments. "Thank you."

"I wasn't finished. Your beauty is hard to ignore. Hell, Jolie, you pack a punch. Even a blind man would be able to see it. I suspect many people have stopped there, simply because of the force of what you are. But" – Ted raised a finger when Jolie started to speak – "but they'd be stupid to stop there. Beauty is one thing, but that fades with age. The other stuff I see? That's the good stuff. You have an agile mind. You remember stories and myths in intricate detail. You're friendly; sometimes beautiful women can be bitchy or competitive with other women, but I've never seen that in you. You're kind to all, nice and welcoming, and you clearly have the respect of most people on the island, since they've trusted you with their stories. You're adventurous, a risk-taker, willing to try new things like taking a job when a random professor offers one, and you create a beautiful home for people to enjoy. There are so many more layers to you, Jolie. Don't ever let anyone just value you on beauty alone."

"I... oh, there I go..." Jolie laughed as tears dripped down her face. She wanted to hug him, to just climb into his lap and hug him close so she could be cradled in his words forever.

Ted muttered something else and then looked away.

"What was that? I missed it." Jolie looked up.

"And, much to my chagrin, you can even drive a fricking boat!"

She laughed the whole way to their mooring.

CHAPTER 25

"This is Nalachi's reef?" Ted asked. He'd very politely allowed Jolie to collect her emotions. She'd not even felt compelled to compliment him back, which was a true gift in her opinion. Many times people only gave compliments to hear compliments in return, but Ted's observations were genuine, with no trace of ulterior motives to them.

"It is," Jolie said, having cut the engine. She'd instructed Ted on how to hook the mooring line with the pole at the front of the boat. And maybe she'd admired his butt when he bent to lean out over the water and grab the rope floating by the buoy. It was hard not to look – he was *really* well put-together.

"Will you tell me about it? From here?" Ted asked, looking down into the water.

"I'll tell you about it from above and then show you it below."

"Below? We're going in?"

"Of course we're going in. Don't you want to see the reef?"

"I mean, of course, but – well, okay," Ted said and crossed his arms over his chest.

"Ted. Can you swim?" Jolie belatedly realized she had assumed he would want to go in the water.

"Yes, I can. I'm a strong swimmer actually. I'm just not the best snorkeler."

"Ah, okay. Tell me why?"

"I can never seem to figure out the snorkel and the mask part. My mask always fogs up and my snorkel always gets water in it and then I end up choking and it's never fun for anyone."

That was twice today that she'd seen him flustered, Jolie realized. It was kind of nice to see that he wasn't coolly confident in every situation.

"I have solutions to those problems, if you're willing to give it a chance."

"I trust you," Ted said, and warmth flooded Jolie again.

"And knowing your love of documenting things, I've even brought an underwater camera."

"See? Smart," Ted said.

Jolie beamed at him. "Let's start from the surface," she said. "Then, because it's roasting out, we'll have a nice relaxing cool-off in the water and then some lunch. Does that work for you?"

"Perfect."

"Okay, Professor, listen up. I've already told you Nalachi and Irmine's story, so all of that remains the same. But what I'm showing you today is how tricky the reef is here and why Nalachi made the mistake he did. Granted, he was blinded by love when he was paddling out in his boat, but he was still a seasoned fisherman and should have looked for the signs of the reef."

"Where the darker spots are?" Ted said, leaning over the side of the boat to study the water.

"Yes. See here, here, and over there? The darker spots indicate rocks or reef under the water. The brilliant turquoise indicates a stretch of sand, where it's not likely for your hull to scrape anything. Now, look over here." Jolie pointed to a slightly darker spot, but not as dark as the others.

"What's that?"

"Still reef. But due to the color of the corals on top, it's not as dark. But can you see how the water catches on it? Where there are little ripples and sometimes even white-caps to the waves hitting it? There's something beneath that's disturbing the natural flow of the water."

"That one's much trickier to see," Ted admitted.

"Exactly. Even experienced sailors would have to be careful. Most would steer clear of this whole area, because they'd see that it's a patchy area. Depending on the size of their boat, many wouldn't even come in this far."

"But Nalachi just had his small fishing boat."

"Right. And as the storm was whipping up, he was also losing control. That's another factor to consider. Even if he'd wanted to stay away from the reef, sometimes we aren't in control of all the factors of our destiny." As she looked down at the water, Jolie wondered if she was speaking to herself.

"It's a sad story. But also a romantic one. I find that

many romantic stories can be quite tragic. The two often go hand-in-hand," Ted murmured, straightening up.

"It's true. It was tragic, and heartbreaking for those involved. But at the same time, the love endures. And I have to believe, above all else, that love is worth dying for. It's the one thing in this world that you'll feel through the centuries… it's the only thing that perseveres, really. Love."

"I can almost feel it," Ted admitted, looking down to the water and then back up at the mermaid statue, searching for her mate. "It's powerful here, in this place."

"There's love here. There's death and tragedy. But the love is what holds."

"I think I'm ready for you to show me below the water. If you really do have a solution for my issues. I can't help but want to see if I can feel the same… current of power beneath the waves."

"Now, how can you tell me you don't believe in magick, but you can feel currents of love and the power of it all here?" Jolie demanded, hands on her hips. When Ted's mouth dropped open in surprise, she added, "Sorry, I didn't mean to spring that on you. I'm just trying to understand."

"No, it's a fair question. I just hadn't thought about it. Maybe… I think my feelings of a place" – Ted held a hand to his chest – "those are my interpretations of the image and scenario my mind's creating around the stories you weave."

"You think what you're feeling is because your mind has created it?" Jolie asked.

"I do, yes. It doesn't lessen the power of all this, at all. It's just how I'm understanding it."

"So, no magick?"

"Um... not yet, I guess." Ted gave her a crooked grin, and Jolie smiled back.

She couldn't force it on him, she knew that. But part of her wanted to smack him upside the head and make a believer of him.

"Okay, solutions," Jolie said, and dug in the gear she'd brought with her. "First, I have a snorkel with wave protection on it. So long as you keep your face in the water and your snorkel angled up, no water will get in. If you roll your head all the way to your chest and try to look down by your feet, then yes, you'll dip your snorkel in the water and flood it."

"Got it. Face down."

"Secondly, I have drops for your mask to help with the cloudiness. This isn't a new mask, so the film has been burned off. Typically, brand new masks have a film on them. Most people don't realize that and take their masks out snorkeling, then can't see through the fog."

"Ahh, that's sneaky."

"It's always best to treat a new mask first. Either with toothpaste swiped on it or burning it with a lighter."

"I did not know this."

"I don't suspect you're doing much snorkeling in Boston."

"That I am not."

"Next, I'm giving you a pool noodle." Jolie pulled out a long Styrofoam noodle and handed it to him.

"Why?" Ted demanded, looking at the noodle in shock.

"Because it keeps you lying horizontal, so you don't dip your snorkel in the water, and you don't have to think about doing a bunch of things at once. You can just float on it and look down at the reef."

"But I can swim, Jolie. I feel like you're giving me water wings."

"I'm just taking one element out of the picture for you. Then all you have to focus on is breathing and looking at the fish."

"Fine, but I'm accepting this only because my research assistant insists. I don't need to lose any man points here," Ted said as he stripped off his shirt.

Jolie's mouth went dry. Oh, he was definitely not going to lose any man points, that was for sure. She'd only seen him with his shirt off once before, and that had been in the moonlight. Now, in the light of day, she could see just how fit he was. It took everything in her power to turn away and not reach out and run her hands down his chest.

"No man points lost. And I promise to not send any photos to your colleagues. But I will keep them for my negotiation strategy regarding my royalty percentage in this book of yours. Now that I'm writing a chapter and all."

"You drive a hard bargain, Jolie."

"If you only knew." Jolie smiled and did a backward dive off the boat, smiling at the shocked look on Ted's face before the water submerged over her and welcomed her home.

CHAPTER 26

"*N*ow you're just showing off," Ted said when she surfaced. He looked like a child, grumpily holding his pool noodle and mask.

"You seem cranky. Better get in the water and cool off," Jolie said, laughing up at him, then shrieked when he cannonballed into the ocean, splashing water all over her face.

"Do men ever grow up?" Jolie asked when he surfaced, sputtering saltwater. She quickly swam to retrieve his pool noodle, which had drifted away, then returned to where he was treading water. "Okay, mask on, Dr. Macalister."

"Why is everyone so obsessed with the 'doctor' part of my name here?"

"It's just fun to say. And I like your last name."

"Thank you," Ted said and put the mask on his face, pulling the strap way too tight at the back of his head. "Ouch."

"Not so tight," Jolie said, and swam over to adjust it

for him. Once it was more comfortable, she angled the snorkel correctly and handed him his noodle.

"Where's your mask?"

"I don't need one."

"How so? It's saltwater."

"It doesn't burn my eyes. Years of swimming in it, I guess." Jolie shrugged. "Okay, put the pool noodle under your chest."

Ted did as she instructed.

"Face in the water and don't kick anywhere, just breathe."

Jolie watched as he went from tense to relaxed as he chilled out on the pool noodle, looking down at the variety of fish that swam below them. Dragging his noodle with her, she tugged him closer to the spot she really wanted to show him. Luckily, with his face in the water and the snorkel in, Ted didn't raise his head to ask any questions about her ability to see in the water.

They floated that way for a while, gently kicking in the water while Jolie pointed out various things for Ted to look at. When he didn't see the eel poking out from a coral head, she let go of him and swam gently to the reef and pointed, turning to look up at him and smile so he could see. When a turtle swam over the top of the coral head, she beckoned to it like she normally would; it swam right over to her, bumping its nose against her face before heading to the surface to breathe. Turning in the water, she saw Ted's shocked look and realized she'd better surface for air as most humans would.

"How did you –" Ted asked, pulling the snorkel from

his mask as she broke the surface of the water "– how did you hold your breath that long?"

"I'm a freediver," Jolie said, her eyes meeting his.

"A freediver?"

"Yes; instead of scuba diving with tanks, you freedive. One breath of air. It takes a lot of training, actually. You have to meditate a bit too. It's amazing what people can do when they're trained."

"But that turtle came right up to you."

"Wasn't he cute?"

"Well, yeah. Adorable. But is that normal?"

"Depends on the turtle. Some are friendly. Some don't want to be bothered."

"I'm in awe. You didn't even take a photo."

"Oh, I'm sorry. I forgot. I'll take a picture if I see another."

"Can I see the camera? Is it a point and shoot?"

"Yes, very simple." Jolie handed it over and showed him how it worked.

"Do you mind if I try some photos?"

"Not at all."

"If you can find anything else for me to see, let me know. It's all kind of a blur of color and interesting things so if you can point anything out, I'm interested."

"I'll do that."

Jolie spent the next thirty minutes diving down to the reef to point out sea life for Ted. She found him a lobster, a stingray, a variety of eels, and even a few more turtles who were kind enough to swim over and say hello. He seemed content to take photos from above and Jolie enjoyed showing him the ocean life she was so passionate about.

Finally, though, they came close to the spot she'd brought him here for. Surfacing, she poked him in the arm.

"This is incredible, Jolie. Really. Thank you for sharing it with me."

"You're welcome. This is my happy place. I love the reefs and watching all the fish. Each coral head is like its own little village."

"I can see why. I feel like I could be out here for days and never notice time going by."

"Are you ready for what I wanted to show you here? Most people don't get to see this."

"I can't wait," Ted said, smiling at her. He looked like such a dork in his mask and snorkel, and yet still managed to be cute.

"Okay, just stay horizontal on your noodle. I'm going to pull you through kind of a narrow little channel."

"Aye, aye, captain." Ted saluted.

Jolie tugged his noodle – her immature side snickering at the phrase in her head – and pulled him through a narrow channel where the reef came almost to the top of the water on both sides. True to his word, Ted stayed still and let Jolie tow him through so that neither of them hurt the coral. Once through, she turned and pointed down to what she'd brought him here to see. Immediately, his head popped out of the water.

"Jolie! Is that…"

"Yes, it's another statue. Unknown to most."

Ted didn't respond. He just plunked his head back in the water and began taking photos while Jolie swam in lazy circles around the statue in the sand on the ocean floor. The reef formed almost a perfect circle around the statue, and unless someone swam to it, they'd never find this hidden gem.

The statue showcased the mermaid, once again entwined around her human man, as they lovingly embraced each other. It was the same carving on the comb Ted had found, the necklace the oracle had given him in his dream, and the rock wall of the cave she'd taken him to. This was the full embodiment of the design, showing the love in all its glory, with smooth lines and intricate details etched into the stone. Jolie visited it often, drawn to it around the full moon, and it had become a sacred meditation area for her people. Those who came to visit this statue came to celebrate love in all its forms – for even in her community, a mermaid choosing a human partner had not always been accepted. It was a fight against the odds, the epitome of love conquering all, and a shrine to those who had lost everything to stand for what was most important.

The mermaid stood, her head at a haughty angle, as she cradled her lover in her arms, with no apologies for her choices. Surrounded by pristine white sand and a perfect circle of reef teeming with a rainbow of fish at the edges, the spot never ceased to bring Jolie to a point of deep contemplation. No one who visited here would ever leave untouched.

Jolie watched as Ted paddled about at the surface, taking pictures from different angles, completely absorbed in the beauty he saw below. She looked from him to the statue and back. Maybe Irma was right. It was time to be honest with him about her feelings. The worst he could say was no, right? Even the thought of it sent a shudder through Jolie. She'd need to work herself up to that, she supposed, but glancing back at the couple depicted in the statue, she realized that love was worth taking risks for.

"Jolie!" Ted popped his head up and she swam over to him.

"Cool, huh?"

"I'd say more than cool. Jolie – this is a masterpiece. Truly a work of great art. This should be in a museum."

"It's already in a museum," Jolie said, raising her hand to the sky and gesturing to the ocean around them. She couldn't imagine a museum ever creating a more perfect spot for this statue than where it currently sat.

"But… so many more people could enjoy this beautiful artwork."

"Does art have to be validated by millions of people seeing it? Is it any less beautiful if only a rare few get to glimpse it?"

"I… no, you're right. That doesn't detract from its beauty, no."

"Then I'd argue that it's even more powerful because of its location. Taking it out of here could cheapen it to just another mermaid statue."

"Nothing could cheapen this. It's exquisite. But I understand what you're saying. I guess I was thinking that more is always better."

"More people would ruin the impact of this. Visiting this spot? Well, it's a gift." Jolie splashed some water at him lightly. "And it's time for us to go; the tides are changing."

"I'll follow your lead. Thank you for bringing me here. Dare I say it's magickal?"

"Now you're beginning to see the light."

"Maybe I just need to drink the Kool-Aid," Ted murmured.

Jolie glanced back at him in confusion as she began to swim them out of there. "I don't understand."

"Oh… it's a joke referencing a cult. It's a long story."

"You're saying magick is a cult?"

"No, not at all. It's just a phrase we use when talking about people who blindly follow things that don't make sense."

Jolie stopped and turned, treading water once again as she studied him.

"Nobody's pushing you, Ted. You believe or you don't. This is your choice. It isn't for me to make a decision for you or to twist your arm."

"Ah, I see I've misspoken again. Please, I don't mean to offend. Thank you for bringing me here. It's one of the loveliest things I've ever had the pleasure to lay eyes on."

Placated, Jolie turned and swam them out of the channel and toward the boat. But the whole time her thoughts whirled in her head. Just when she'd almost convinced herself to tell Ted how she really felt and show him who she was, he'd likened magick to a cult.

Unsure of how to proceed, Jolie decided to tuck that decision away for another day.

CHAPTER 27

They had a picnic. Jolie had brought enough food to feed four people, and laid it out prettily on a towel beneath the shade covering of the boat. Ted watched her motions, buzzing about in the smallest slip of a bikini he'd ever seen, moving confidently around the boat and chattering away about the different types of fish she'd pointed out to him. Had he died and gone to heaven? Who was this fearless woman who could walk around all but naked without blinking an eye, had a seemingly encyclopedic knowledge of mermaid mythology, and now, apparently, was also some sort of underwater biologist?

It was becoming increasingly hard for Ted to separate his personal feelings for Jolie from his professional ones. It would be best, he scolded himself once again, if he put some distance between them soon.

"Jolie, this is perfect. Thank you for bringing the lunch. I'll be sure to compensate you for it."

"Why? That's what friends do."

"Ah, but this was a business trip. As such, the boss

should pay." Ted could have sworn he saw a trace of sadness cross her beautiful face and he held up a hand. "Okay – as friends then, the next outing is on me."

"That's fair," Jolie said, grabbing a grape and popping it into her mouth. They sat in silence for a bit, letting the boat rock gently under them, while Ted took a sip of his crisp white wine and studied the mermaid statue.

"How do they change?"

"Excuse me?" Jolie glanced over at him.

"The mermaids. How does it work, do you think?"

"Well…" Jolie shot a cheeky grin at him.

"Okay, fine, I get it. Magick."

"It is magick. It's not like they have a tail that folds up into their butt or something and flips out when they feel like it."

"Okay, that's a very uncomfortable image," Ted laughed, taking another sip of his wine and stretching out his legs on the cushion in front of him. Sun glittered across the blue water, and birds swooped down by the boat where Jolie tossed a few scraps for them to eat.

"Isn't it? Honestly, from what I understand, it's just a simple incantation they use. But it comes from here." Jolie held her fist to her core. "And I think some can only change at the full moon, while others can change at whim."

"Is there an origin story for the mermaids of Siren Island? What's the tie with the full moon?"

"An origin story?"

"Sure. Most cultures have sort of a beginning story of how mermaids came to be. Kind of like Adam and Eve in the Bible. Does Siren Island have one? I haven't yet found anything about that."

"Ah, okay, sure. I know it."

"You do?" Ted sat up and reached for his pack. "Can you tell me? Can I record you?"

"Of course." Jolie shrugged one shoulder delicately. She was so beautiful in that moment, with her hair tumbling wild about her and the turquoise waters behind her, that Ted almost gave in to his very real desire to kiss her. Instead, he turned away and took a breath to calm himself down.

"I should have asked you sooner. I've been scouring the few books that Maureen gave me from her shop, but to no avail."

"Best to ask your research assistant and co-author. She probably knows." Jolie stuck her chin up in the air and he grinned at her, enjoying how much she was taking to her new role.

"You could write the whole book. Your knowledge is impeccable. Maybe you should write it and I'll just write the foreword."

"Really? You think I could write a book?"

"Of course you could. You're excellent at storytelling. Why not try writing?"

"Because I've never taken any classes for it."

"So? Write what you want. Then you get an editor to help you figure it out."

"Just like that?"

"Why not? You won't know unless you try."

"I could say the same for you." Jolie laughed and then waved a hand at him. "Okay, you're distracting me. So, you want to hear the origin story of the Siren Island mermaids?"

"Very much so."

"It involves a lot of magick."

"As it should."

"No judgment then."

"None. Promise." Ted held his hand to his heart and Jolie settled back against a cushion, pushing her tumble of curls over her shoulder and staring out to sea. Even though he had said he'd record her voice, Ted hit video record on his phone. He wanted this moment to watch for the rest of his life.

"Ages ago, when the earth was still figuring things out, the worlds blended a little differently. Gods and goddesses walked easily among men, and were revered as rulers and peacemakers. There were rulers of the sky, the earth, and the oceans. The worlds overlapped, as did the magick found in each. You may have heard of one of the great rulers of the ocean, Poseidon?"

"Of course," Ted said.

"Poseidon ruled all the oceans. Not just the Caribbean Sea or the Atlantic; he was all-powerful. Now, our dear Poseidon had a bit of a crush, you see. It was on the goddess who ruled the night skies, one of the few who had power and pull over his oceans. Because while he ruled his oceans, our lovely Selene, Goddess of the Moon, ruled the tides.

"Poseidon became quite captivated with our lovely Selene, and she, in turn, with him. They struck up a great love affair, and it was a glorious unity between the oceans and the skies. Together, there was harmony of the worlds.

They looked to the humans that ruled the land, and realized perhaps there was a way to... to upgrade the humans and make them sort of a trifecta of power. I'm not sure if I'm explaining that right." Jolie laughed at herself.

"You're saying they wanted to create a perfect hybrid human who could exist on land and sea."

"Right. But I always wondered – why not flight, too? With Selene being of the skies, wouldn't she want these new beings to fly as well? Ah, well; she was a bit vain so perhaps she didn't want them flying too close to her."

"Or she wanted a slight upper hand over Poseidon."

"That also makes sense; he was very overbearing. Anyway, they designed a creature of both land and sea, and bred many of them, their children together. In the beginning they kept them to the waters until Selene felt they were ready to show the people of the land what beauty had come of their union. Certain they would be accepted, Selene and Poseidon encouraged their children to go to land and show themselves."

"I'm guessing it did not go well."

"It did not. Instead of being welcoming, the humans sought to kill that which they did not understand. The mermaids were destroyed, hunted as witches and devil beasts. The ones who survived retreated deep into the waters while Poseidon unleashed his fury on the humans and Selene wept for her children."

"The great floods."

"Correct. When the dust settled, centuries later, the mermaids still existed but had grown shy of humans. You see, the humans never tried to befriend them or learn about them. They only saw that the mermaids were different, and therefore must be evil. What could have been a beautiful friendship between land and sea ended up being disastrous, because the humans could have used the mermaids' help, if only they'd reacted with kindness."

"And the mermaids didn't seek revenge?"

"Why would they? They knew they were more powerful. There was no point to it. The mermaids didn't have to flex their strength to prove anything; they simply no longer allowed humans into their world."

"And nothing has changed?"

"And that's the way they've kept it. The mermaids continued to grow and build their society, and occasionally they befriend a human who they can sense is kind. They're curious, you know? It's why they go up to fishermen. Mermaids have bountiful hearts, and they're always looking for the good. It's only when humans have turned on them and they've had to protect themselves that they've become dangerous."

"The stories of sirens luring men to their death?"

"Mmm, I can't say that there haven't been a few rogue mermaids over the years who were particularly nasty. Usually it's because they're hurting over a broken heart."

"So Irmine could have turned nasty?" Ted nodded to the statue.

"She could have. She was broken-hearted. But instead, she chooses to warn sailors away from the reefs so others don't have to know her pain."

"She had a good heart."

"Yes."

"So when the full moon comes…"

"Selene invites her children out to play."

"And that's why the mermaids are most often seen at that time."

"Exactly."

"That's quite a story. Thank you for sharing it with me. It's like one of the fairy tales my mom used to read me as a child."

"Are you close to your family?" Jolie asked, reaching for a slice of cheese.

"I am. My parents travel a lot. They hunkered down in Vermont for decades and then decided to be nomads. My sister still lives in Vermont; she's an apprentice in a glass-blowing shop there."

"A glass-blowing shop? That sounds fun."

"It's hot work. But gratifying for her. I'm not sure I'd be able to create like she does."

"But you do now, with your lesson plans and what you tell your students. And now, your book."

"Right, my book." Ted shook his head as bubbly lightness filled him at the thought. "My book. My very own book. It sounds good, doesn't it?"

"It does. Dr. Theodore Macalister, author."

"Oof, that makes me nervous." Ted laughed, rubbing a hand across his stomach.

"There's time for nerves later. After the book is done. Don't talk yourself out of it before you've even started."

"Thank you." Ted measured a look at Jolie. "You're incredibly kind, you know that?"

"Not always. I can be quite snarky, I've been told."

"That's just your dry wit. I don't think you truly intend to be mean."

"No, I don't like hurting people's feelings unless they hurt mine."

"Have you been hurt before?"

"Honestly? Not truly. I've never let someone get close enough."

"Scared? I get that. I think I've been the same way." Ted held up the wine bottle and poured them each another glass.

"No string of broken hearts behind you?"

"Mmm, no not really. I've never been that guy. All my relationships have ended amicably."

"Amicably. No tears? No fights?" Jolie shot him a look.

"No, not really."

"It sounds like there was more friendship than passion."

"Well... yeah, I guess you're right."

"What a pair we are," Jolie laughed.

"Nevertheless, here we are. And not a bad way to spend a day, right?"

"No, this is an easy kind of day. Do you really want to camp at the beach?" Jolie turned to look at Ted again.

"I'd love nothing more. Are we going mermaid hunting?"

"Um, how about we call it mermaid seeking? Hunting implies taking them out."

"Right, right – bad use of language there. Yes, I'd love to. Do you think we'll spot one?"

"One hundred percent," Jolie murmured and turned her head to look at the statue of Irmine far above them.

CHAPTER 28

$\mathcal{T}$ ed lay in bed that night, replaying the video of Jolie telling the story over and over. He memorized the curve of her lips, the way her face lit up when she talked about something she was passionate about, and how her hair exploded in a cloud of curls down her back.

His heart ached for her.

Unable to sleep, he stuck the memory card of the little underwater camera that Jolie had lent him into the computer and downloaded the photos he'd taken. It had awed him the way she'd dropped effortlessly to the ocean floor, peeking amongst the corals, and turning to point things out to him. He'd never seen anything like it, and had been shocked at how long she could hold her breath.

On a hunch, he googled what the longest breath-hold underwater was.

"Twenty-two minutes!" Ted exclaimed and looked up at the ceiling. So this was actually a thing, he realized, and began researching freediving. A half-hour later, with newfound respect for Jolie, he opened the folder to look at the images he'd taken.

The first one showed her curvy body floating across the ocean floor, her head turned to smile at him, hair streaming in a cloud down her back. If ever there was a mermaid, Ted mused. He was struck once again by her eyes being open in the saltwater. Flipping back to his free-diving research, he noted that every image showed a diver wearing a mask.

"That's odd," Ted said, and started researching salt water and vision. It turned out, though, that many people could adjust to seeing underwater if they allowed the stinging of the saltwater to settle. Ted then spent another fascinating half-hour reading up on the sea nomads, a tribe of people who lived in the Andaman Sea. Their children were known to be able to see underwater, as they spent many hours a day fishing for clams and crustaceans in the sea. It turned out the children could adapt their eyes to see better even in the salt water. Maybe one day he'd take a trip there – if they allowed visitors – and learn if they had their own mermaid myths. It seemed like a colony of sea nomads would be likely to have some really interesting stories.

"So much to learn…" Ted mused and went back to flicking through the photos he'd taken earlier that day. He'd meant to take photos of all the fish and wildlife that Jolie was showing him, but he realized now that his focus had been elsewhere.

On her.

Shot after shot reflected Jolie in all her confidence and beauty. As he flipped through them, faster and faster, his eyes began to play tricks on him – for a moment, he thought he saw a mermaid tail. Stopping on that photo, he stared as hard as he could, but to no avail. It was only Jolie – though she looked as much like a mermaid as a human could, he supposed.

He needed to get a hold on his emotions. It wouldn't do to be lusting after an employee and Irma's daughter. Every day, as his attraction grew, Ted berated himself for having thoughts outside the boundaries he had set. Even more troublesome was the fact that women like Jolie did not end up with men like Ted. Women like Jolie were meant for fancy yachts and being draped in diamonds and rich silks, their every need catered to, with exclusive invitations to the biggest parties in the world. Women like Jolie would not be interested in his stuffy department dinners and long cold nights in Boston. She was so far out of his league they weren't even playing the same game.

Ted carefully erased the photos from the memory card, not wanting Jolie to find them and think he was a creep, and shut his laptop. Leaning back against his pillows, he squeezed the bridge of his nose. Was the island getting to him? Here he was, half-convinced that Jolie was a mermaid, and that magick was real. It was becoming increasingly difficult to keep an objective viewpoint, when story after story from locals told him that mermaids actually existed.

Maybe that was the true magick of Siren Island – it allowed people, if even for just a moment, to believe.

CHAPTER 29

*J*olie found both Mirra and Irma in the kitchen in the morning, the windows thrown open to encourage the breeze and a heaping stack of pancakes piled on a platter in the middle of the table.

"I hope you're hungry," Mirra said, laughing at her over the pancakes.

"Famished. These look delicious."

"They are. I added a touch of cinnamon today," Irma said.

Jolie poured herself a glass of mango juice and grabbed a plate. Settling herself at the table, she piled her plate full and dug in. They all ate in companionable silence for a while, Bob Dylan singing a rambling tune in the background, and Jolie felt some of her tension ease. Once the worst of her hunger was sated, she pushed her plate back and looked up.

"Ready to talk?" Irma asked, sipping her coffee from a mermaid mug.

"I'm going to tell him," Jolie said.

Mirra reached across the table to squeeze Jolie's hand. "Oh, I'm so happy for you." A sheen of tears flooded Mirra's eyes.

"Don't you start. If you start, then I'll go. I don't know what he's going to say."

"Well, of course he'll be happy. What man wouldn't want you?"

"You know, I take back all the nasty things I've said about you."

Mirra stuck her tongue out at Jolie. "What exactly do you plan to tell him, Jolie?"

"That's what I want to talk to you about."

"We already told you we trust your judgment about whether you tell him about us," Mirra said.

"He's a fine young man, Jolie. I trust him," Irma said.

"First, I want to tell him I have feelings for him. You're both right. I need to stop waiting for the man to take the lead. I've gotten so used to men lusting after me that I'm completely out of the habit of making the first move."

"But this is more than lust," Mirra said softly.

"It is…" Jolie sighed and stabbed another bit of pancake with her fork.

"Is it because the oracle said he was for you? Are you pushing back against that?" Irma asked.

"Initially, a bit, yes. I don't like to be told what to do."

"I'm shocked." Mirra feigned a surprised look.

"And I was worried that the magick of her words was clouding my actual emotions."

"But you no longer feel that way?"

"No, I don't. I've really spent some time thinking about this. And we've spent a lot of time together over these last several weeks. He's a good man. Like, a really, really, good man. An honorable one. He's smart, and funny, and so very handsome. I... well... I love him." Jolie looked up at that and Mirra fanned her face to stop the tears from falling.

"Jolie, I'm so happy for you." Irma leaned over and pressed a kiss to her cheek. "I have wanted this for you."

"What about me?" Mirra demanded, looking like an angry angel in her white dress and annoyed expression.

"For *both* of you," Irma corrected with a smile.

"But I worry he doesn't feel the same."

"You won't know if you don't ask."

"Yes, that's what it's going to take. No matter how many signals I throw at the man, he's oblivious."

"I doubt he's oblivious," Mirra said.

"No, he isn't. He watches her." Irma nodded to Mirra and they both turned and smiled at Jolie.

"He does? He really does?"

"Oh yeah, constantly. He's always sneaking looks in your direction. When he talks in a group, he often directs the conversation to you. He's engaged with you. He likes you, whether he'll allow himself to admit it or not."

"Okay, that makes me feel a bit better," Jolie breathed. She took a sip of her juice, her mind skipping to her preparations for tonight.

"Will you show him who you are?"

"I plan to. I don't think we could ever have a true relationship if I didn't."

"Are you worried how he'll respond?"

"No, not really. In all honesty, I think he'll be thrilled. He's wanted to see a mermaid for so long now."

"Oh, I'm so excited for you both." Mirra clapped her hands together. "Okay, let's get down to planning. We need to pick outfits. And what are you bringing for dinner?"

"He said food is on him since I brought lunch yesterday for the boat. Oh! And get this: He's going to write a book."

"Is he? That's awesome," Mirra exclaimed.

"And, even more fun, he asked me to write the fore-word for it." Jolie glanced at Irma and Mirra, waiting for them to tease her.

"Oh, Jolie. That's fantastic news! I'm so proud of you. You do have a delightful way with words," Irma said, beaming at Jolie.

"My sister – the author!" Mirra laughed. "This is perfect."

"Wait, you don't think it's silly?"

"No, why would it be silly? You have a brilliant brain. I'm excited to see what you put together. Why, we could even put the books in the guestrooms here."

Jolie tuned out as Irma and Mirra began to chatter about where to put the as-yet-unwritten book, and her heart filled with hope. Maybe, just maybe, she'd finally find the love she'd dreamed of.

CHAPTER 30

*J*olie straightened at a knock at her bedroom door. She'd just gotten out of the shower, and had selected a particularly sexy bra and underwear set in midnight blue satin. Figuring it was Mirra, she strode to the door and opened it.

"I'm just picking out my outfit if you want to..." Her voice trailed off as she registered Ted's shocked face standing at the door. "Oh, I thought you were Mirra."

"No..." Ted's voice came out sounding like he was choking. Jolie hid her smile, feeling heat flash through her, as she sauntered over to the bathroom door where her robe hung, knowing full well the view her thong underwear provided as she did so.

"If this is a bad time," Ted said, and when she turned around she found him with his back turned and talking out to the empty hallway.

"Ted, I'm decent. This has more coverage than the bikini I wore yesterday." Jolie laughed at him as he turned.

"I know, I know. I'm just trying to not be a creep, you know?"

"What can I help you with, Ted?"

"I realized I don't have your phone number."

"Are you asking me for my number?"

"I just… I mean, I wanted to see if there was anything else I can help you with for tonight. I have all the food and refreshments sorted, as well as a first aid kit, bug spray, kindling for a fire, camp chairs, a battery-operated radio, my camera equipment, and –"

"And a partridge in a pear tree?" Jolie finished for him, laughing when he shrugged sheepishly.

"I like to be prepared."

"I have the tent, a sleeping pad, a few sheets because it's too hot for sleeping bags, and a couple of hammocks if we decide sleeping in a hammock is better." Jolie hoped he'd choose to sleep in the tent next to her, especially after what she planned to tell him tonight, but wanted to leave things open.

"Perfect. Oh, and did you invite Irma and Mirra? I thought they might like to join. It could be a mermaid-seeking party."

"Oh… they have plans. I spoke to them this morning," Jolie lied – but she also knew that there was nothing that would keep Irma and Mirra out of the water on the night of a full moon. More than likely those sneaky bitches would be spying on them from the water, Jolie thought.

"Okay, that's fine then. I didn't want them to feel left out."

"That's very kind of you. If you have fun tonight

maybe we can organize a group camping outing some-where another time."

"That would be fun. It might be nice to see if Prince would come, or some of the other people I've met."

Jolie threw back her head and laughed. "Prince may seem like he's comfortable with hanging out in nature, but that man has grown a little soft in his elder years. He likes the creature comforts, I can promise you that."

"Ah, well, just a thought. Need a hand with loading the supplies up?"

"I put them in the back hallway if you want to grab them. I'll just be a moment longer."

Ted left and Jolie hurried to change. Pulling a simple orange sarong-style skirt from her drawer, she wrapped it around her waist and pulled a flowy navy tank over her head. Foregoing jewelry, she braided her hair back in one long loose braid, and slipped her feet into rugged sandals that would allow her to clamber over the rocks that led to the beach. Not needing anything else, as she planned to be naked or underwater much of the evening, Jolie left her room with a smile hovering on her lips.

"All set? We should be getting there just before sunset, so plenty of time to watch the moonrise."

"All set, captain. Hmm, I feel like we should give you a name for your mission tonight." Jolie smiled her thanks as he held the truck door open for her.

"Captain Mermaid Seeker?"

"Doesn't quite have the ring I had in mind. We'll work on it. Anyway, onward!"

They drove to the beach, not really talking much, instead listening to the reggae music that pulsed through the car. With the windows down, the breeze high, and the sun dropping low in the sky, it was the perfect time of day to cruise the waterfront and head toward the cliffs. Once they were close, Jolie reminded him where to turn, and they rattled their way down the bumpy path until they reached the rocky beach and the cliff's edge.

"I did not plan well for this," Ted said, as he stood by the cliff wall and looked down at the narrow ledge beneath the water that would lead them to the beach. "Why did I bring so much stuff? It'll take ages to bring all this safely across."

"Why don't we start with just the basics and decide later if we need anything else?" Jolie suggested, biting back a smile at the frustration on Ted's face. He clearly was very hard on himself when things didn't go according to plan.

They spent the next twenty minutes hauling gear and food and a few other things across the ledge. Jolie promised him he didn't need to bring the first aid kit, which was half the size of her, and soon she was digging out a hole in the sand for their fire while Ted pitched the tent. He'd already strung the hammocks between a few palm trees, but Jolie had stopped him from bringing camp chairs over. She promised him the sand would be equally as comfortable to sit on.

"I'm surprised you like this stuff," Ted said, coming over to study Jolie's handiwork. Not only had she dug the hole for the fire, she'd created a little teepee of twigs and papers to act as the fire starter.

"What? Fires?"

"No. This. Camping. No fancy beds, no toilets, no showers. No room service."

Jolie angled her head and looked up at him standing over her. "Is that the kind of girl you think I am?"

"You strike me as someone well-suited for a fancy life-style. I could see you on a yacht, dripping in jewels and having cabana boys fawn over you."

"Well, no, I don't suppose I'd say no to that experience either." Jolie laughed, brushing her palms off and standing up. "But that would be just for a treat, or like a little vaca-tion. I can't imagine living my whole life like that. Don't you think it would get boring? Being waited on constantly?"

"I have no idea. I've never had the experience."

"I'm so used to being the one who provides customer service that I'd probably stop the cabana boy from turning down my linens and insist on doing it myself."

"You continually surprise me, Jolie," Ted said, a look she couldn't decipher crossing his face.

"I hope that's a good thing."

"It is. It is. It's just that… you think you have someone pegged, but it goes to show there's always more to learn."

This was the perfect opening, Jolie told herself. Tell him.

"Oh look!" Ted exclaimed and Jolie jumped. "The moon's rising over the cliffs, just as the sun's going down. I need to get a panoramic picture of this. Where did I put my camera?"

"It's in your pack in the tent," Jolie said automatically, letting the moment slide past, telling herself they had all night. For now, she'd let him enjoy the gifts that nature was currently bestowing upon them.

"Come look! This is magnificent!"

"I'll be right there," Jolie said. Taking a breath, she tried to settle her emotions by staring out to the water where the sun was just disappearing below the horizon. For a moment, she spotted Irma popping her head up from the water, and felt the pulse of love magick she pushed to Jolie across the waves.

Filling with courage, Jolie went to meet her love.

CHAPTER 31

"*A*nd they just laughed at you?" Jolie demanded, stabbing her skewer in the air as though she was slicing a sword through a girl.

"They did. And it wasn't the first time," Ted admitted. "I was woefully geeky all through college. I didn't even have my first kiss until my senior year in college."

"No," Jolie gasped, looking at him.

"Yes, seriously. And it was so awkward I dread even remembering it now."

"Well, you seemed to have gained a lot of confidence since then. There's nothing dorky about you now, Dr. Macalister." Jolie smiled at him over the flickering flames of the small bonfire they'd lit.

They'd watched the sunset together, each swinging in their own hammock, as pink rays streaked the sky and a bold rust-colored moon rose over the cliffs. Ted had been beside himself and had spent a few moments filming the spectacle before finally putting down the camera and just allowing himself to be in the moment. Once he'd gotten out of researcher mode and had relaxed, Jolie had broken out the rum punch – not too strong – and they'd cooked vegetable skewers over the open flames.

"It's hard to shake that feeling though," Ted said, leaning forward to poke the tin-foiled potatoes they'd placed in the hot coals over an hour before. "I still often feel like that geeky kid who'll never be good enough."

"You shouldn't," Jolie said, meeting his eyes across the flames. "I think you're amazing."

"Oh, well, that's very sweet of you. I bet you don't have many getting-bullied stories," Ted said, breaking her gaze and looking away. He clearly hadn't believed what she'd said. "Think the mermaids will come soon?"

"Um, maybe," Jolie said, looking out to the water. She'd already seen several, but Ted had been distracted and she didn't call them out.

"How do we search for them?"

He clearly didn't want to dig any further into his past, and Jolie let the moment slide, sighing to herself about the fact that she couldn't seem to work up the courage to just tell him how she really felt. It was a few hours past sunset now, and the moon hung directly over them, bathing their beach in its ethereal light. What moment could be more perfect than this?

Jolie heard it before he did. Just a whisper on the breeze, tickling her ears, and filling her with a deep-seated longing. As the song intensified, Ted dropped his skewer and stood, racing to the water's edge. Jolie stood, following him, the song begging her to show herself to him. It was the oracle, singing her heart out, just over the horizon and unseen to the world. Her song would carry, holding different meanings to those it reached across the waves, and bold choices would be made this evening. It was rare that the oracle herself sang, and Jolie knew the time had run out on avoiding her future.

"Ted," Jolie said, coming to stand by him. He practically vibrated with excitement, searching the horizon, wanting so desperately to see the mermaid. So distracted was he that he hadn't even bothered to pull his recorder out to catch the song. Not that it could be captured by modern technology anyway, but it hadn't even occurred to him.

"Jolie... I can't... this is miraculous," Ted said, grabbing her hand, not even conscious of what he was doing. She allowed it, and they stood there together as the oracle finished her song, the silence following her last note drawing out until Jolie's palm warmed beneath Ted's. Keeping his hand, she turned to him.

"Ted."

"I've never heard something so beautiful in my life," Ted said, his eyes glossy with tears.

"Ted. Look at me," Jolie said.

He looked down at her. "What an incredible moment."

"Ted, I have to tell you something."

"What's wrong? Was that a fake? There's no way that could be a fake. Nothing could make you feel like that," Ted said, belatedly realizing he was holding Jolie's hand and dropping it. "But how could it –"

"Shh." Jolie put her finger on his lips, shocking him into silence. "Ted, I need to tell you something. I... well, I needed to work myself up to it."

"Okay. Is everything okay?"

"I... well, no, it's not, but at the same time, yes, it is."

Jolie took a deep breath, gathering the courage the song had given her, and met his eyes under the moonlight. "You see, Ted, I think you're amazing. It's not just that you're handsome and have these amazing muscles that I want to lick my way down until I make you moan with aching for me." Jolie stopped and fanned herself as the flush of wanting spread through her.

"Jolie –"

"I'm not finished. I also happen to really enjoy your mind. I like talking to you. For hours and hours. I like that you really listen to me. That you see past my looks and pay attention to my mind. I like that you're kind to my family and my friends. You've been open with the locals, never judging, and they've welcomed you because of it. You're patient, you're ethical, and you make me laugh. Goddess above, you've made me laugh more than anyone I've ever met. And a snorting laugh at that! I can't even get over how many times I've been embarrassed around you. The thing is… you're it for me. I want you to be my part-ner. I don't think you even see how perfect we can be together, but I see it. I know it." Jolie touched her hand to her heart. "Ted, I love you."

Ted's mouth dropped open and he stood there, gaping like a fish, as he stared down at Jolie in utter shock. Taking his silence as a good thing, Jolie slid her arms around his neck and kissed him.

Oh, it was a kiss to dazzle the stars, Jolie thought, as excitement coursed through her, all of her pent-up nerves rushing to the surface as she finally explored the mouth she'd been craving to touch for weeks now. He stood there, not touching her, letting her explore before a small groan escaped his lips and his hands dove into her hair. For a moment, he met her kiss with the same intensity and Jolie was completely swept away.

"Jolie... I can't." Ted broke the kiss and gently pulled her arms from around his neck. His chest labored with his breathing and his eyes were hot with lust in his face. While his words said no, everything about his energy screamed yes to her. Confusion filled her as she looked up at him, like a puppy that had just been kicked.

"But why?"

"It's taking advantage of you. You're my employee. You're Irma's daughter. I absolutely can't cross that line."

"Well, then I quit."

"You don't mean that."

"I *do* mean that. You can't ignore what this is, Ted. Tell me you don't feel something for me." Jolie stomped her foot in the sand. "Tell me you don't know that there's something here."

"I..." Ted looked away, breathing hard. "I can't lie."

"You feel it too. You do!" Jolie pointed her finger at him. "But you won't let me in. Why? Why am I not good enough for you?"

"Oh god, Jolie. You're so much better than me. Don't you see that? It's me who's not good enough for *you*," Ted said, raking a frustrated hand through his hair.

"Don't I get to decide who or what is good enough for me? You don't get to tell me that."

"Jolie..." Ted's voice was pained, and Jolie finally looked away, tears blurring her vision as she took a deep breath. There was more to show him before he could really see her. Maybe then he'd understand why they were exactly perfect for each other.

"I need to show you something," Jolie said, reaching to her waistband and untying her skirt. She tossed it up on the beach; her shirt soon followed. Ted looked stricken by what she was certain was the magnificent sight of her in midnight blue satin, and then she peeled those off her body too. Ted's eyes widened and he froze in his spot.

"If there's anything in your pockets that you don't want to get wet, take it out," Jolie instructed, infusing her voice with her siren magick, forcing him to her command. He did so, blinking at her, and stripped off his shirt. "Follow me."

Jolie turned and walked into the dark ocean, the cool water soothing her temper, Mother Moon calming her with her light.

"Jolie," Ted said, his voice desperate at the shoreline. She remembered how nervous he was of dark water.

"Come with me, Ted. You'll be safe. I promise you."

"I don't think this is the time for skinny dipping."

"Come here." Jolie blasted a pulse of siren magick at him and he strode forward. She'd get in trouble with the oracle for forcing his will, as that was a no-no in the mermaid community, but she figured all bets were off when it came to true love.

Ted strode waist deep into the water, his eyes wide, never leaving hers.

"I promised you mermaids tonight, Dr. Theodore Macalister, and now I'm going to make good on the promise. It's time I showed you exactly who I am," Jolie said.

She murmured the incantation that would change her to

her mermaid form. As the magick rolled over her, her legs shifted to a gloriously sparkled tail in brilliant red – her favorite color – and Jolie smiled as Ted's mouth dropped open.

"You're a mermaid," Ted whispered in awe.

"I am. This is the real me, Ted."

"I… I… you're… this is beyond words. You're stunning," Ted gushed.

"Let me invite you into my world, Ted. When I'm through, you can let me know where your heart stands. It's only fair that there are no secrets between us if we're meant to be life partners."

"Jolie… I can't…" Ted looked so flummoxed that she took pity on him.

"Will you let me show you my home?" Jolie asked again, holding out her hand as she swam to him.

"I'd be a fool to say no."

"Then don't be a fool."

"Yes, Jolie. Please show me your world."

With that, Jolie rose and pressed her lips to his once more, blowing a magickal breath into his mouth that would let him swim with her. She pulled him beneath the surface, hoping he would accept her as his mate.

CHAPTER 32

*S*he dove deep, knowing her magick would keep him safe and allow him to see what she could see. The light of the full moon shone into the ocean, creating a glow that allowed her to point to various fish and other creatures as she pulled him toward her home.

In moments they found themselves at an iridescent mother-of-pearl gate, carved to look like flowing sea grass and kelp, and intertwined with glittery shells. Ted's eyes bulged as he took it all in and she smiled at him, pulling him through the gates and into Siren City.

A child, no more than six years old, peeked out from behind a rock. Swimming closer to study them, she tilted her head at Ted, confused, before darting away faster than any fish could swim. She could sense that Ted wanted to talk, but first she would take him through the city to the secure space in the oracle's cottage, where they could converse safely.

Jolie swam forward, waving to mermaids she knew as they all stopped what they were doing to look at her in shock. It had been ages since she'd come all the way down here for a visit, and now with a human? It would be the talk of the city, that was for sure. Jolie didn't care – she needed Ted to see everything before he could give her his final decision on their future together.

Siren City was laid out much like a castle from olden days. The pearly gates they'd just passed through surrounded the city with an intricate magickal system that bounced any sonar or other types of radar off. Any deep ocean explorations that came their way would be gently redirected.

They didn't close the city to the sea life, instead choosing to work seamlessly with the ocean creatures; they all shared in their abundance together. It wasn't uncommon to see mermaids feeding sharks or cuddling up to sleep while one swam protectively nearby. Dolphins were the clowns of the group, always amusing the mermaids with play, and often being engaged for parties as entertainment.

The various parts of the city had different functions. There was a weapon-making area, for Poseidon hadn't forgotten the days of old when war had ravaged his people. There was a medicines area where magick and sea elements were infused to make tonics and elixirs as needed. Food was foraged through underwater gardening. Jolie's particularly favorite area, the adornment shop, was where everything from glittery shell bras to stunning head-dresses were concocted from every material imaginable. Mermaids scoured the ocean, bringing home the treasures they found, and the adornment department would take these pieces and turn them into miraculous necklaces or delicate tiaras. If there was one thing mermaids loved, it was to sparkle their way through life.

At the head of the city was the castle. Unlike typical castles in the human world, where only the king and queen might reside, all the mermaids lived there. While there was some order to their society, they didn't have a hierarchy so much as roles. Every mermaid played a role, and every mermaid had a voice. Together, they kept their city thriving and healthy, and everyone supported each other in their goals.

Only the oracle lived apart, for she needed to remain objective. For her, they'd set up a marvelous cottage built of hammered ship's gold and dainty shells, and she was content to spend her days there working her magick and reading the lines of fate. This was where Jolie pulled Ted – to the oracle's cottage, knowing he would be safe to speak there. At the threshold, Jolie bowed, and waited for the pulse of magick that would allow them through.

Once inside, Jolie waited while the water drained out, the magickal spell she'd requested taking hold and creating a safe space for Ted to speak. He looked around, his eyes wide, and his mouth slammed closed before meeting her eyes.

"You can breathe here. It's magick. It won't make sense to you, but you're safe."

"Jolie… I feel like I'm hallucinating," Ted breathed.

"It's a little much, isn't it?" Jolie mused, swimming away from him. The water had only drained to their waist, so Jolie could keep her tail, and she moved to the other side of the room and waited to see what he would say.

"I don't even know how to process everything I'm

seeing. It honestly feels like that one time I took shrooms at a Phish concert in college."

"So you don't believe me?"

"I don't know what to think. I can't even understand what's happening."

"You think I drugged you?"

"No, I truly don't think you would do that." Ted turned in a circle, his hair plastered to his head, examining the insides of the cottage. "But maybe the fruit in the rum punch was soured or something? There has to be an explanation."

He still didn't get it, she realized, her heart dropping into her stomach. If she could show him all this and his brain still refused to believe, then there was nothing more she could do.

"This is our home, Ted. I won't apologize or try to defend it. I wanted to share it with you so you could see all parts of me," Jolie said, her chin high and her arms crossed over her chest.

"I... listen, I thank you for that. I truly, truly do. I'm just... I'm struggling. This is mind-blowing. Beyond belief. How is this real?" Ted poked his finger into the water at his waist and looked around again. His eyes were wide and he was breathing heavily, and Jolie realized he was close to panic. Maybe it hadn't been smart to bring him here, she realized. He was a planner, someone who needed to check everything off his list. Shocking him like this might have been a bad move. As he began to gulp for air, she realized the error of her ways.

"Ted, just breathe." Jolie swam to him. "I'm going to

kiss you and give you breath. Take it in and I will bring us safely home."

"But… we're so deep. The pressure. It can't… there's no way. My lungs will pop. I can't take in air this deep and go up," Ted gasped, his shoulders bowing. She gripped him and forced her lips onto his, breathing into his lungs as his terrified eyes met hers. He left her no choice: Jolie put him under, closing his eyes with her hands and pulling him beneath the surface of the water. Swimming from the cabin, she dragged him with her.

She passed the oracle on her way out.

"Trust, Jolie."

"I can't. He won't see me."

"He will. Trust in him."

Jolie kept swimming, refusing to give the oracle any more of herself. She swam straight to the surface, not wanting to delay the inevitable. When they breached the surface, Jolie pulled Ted close until she could deposit his body on the beach, then slipped back, treading water as she took the magick from him and allowed him to waken.

Ted sat up, gasping for breath, clawing at his neck as he looked wildly around. His eyes locked on hers and she held them, refusing to apologize for what she was.

"Jolie… did I pass out?"

"Nope," Jolie said, flipping her tail above the water so he could see it clearly in the moonlight, the red glittering like a bed of rubies.

"Oh god." Ted rolled over on all fours before standing and walking waist-deep toward her.

"Surprise," Jolie said softly.

"I'm having a hard time with this…"

"I see that."

"Why didn't you tell me?"

"Right, because you've been so open to magick? How many times did I tell you magick existed? How many times did you not believe?"

"I... maybe you're right," Ted said, shaking his head. "God, Jolie. Just look at you. You're magnificent."

The moonlight began to dance around them, bouncing around like little shimmery butterflies, and Ted looked up.

"What's happening?"

"Mother Moon is sending you her love."

"Selene?"

"That's correct."

Ted looked up at the moon shimmering in the sky above them. It seemed to do a little dance, like a disco ball turning, its rays shooting down in little spots around them.

"I've never seen anything like this. She's a goddess – shit, Jolie. You're a goddess."

"I am." Jolie thought better of trying to explain the difference between goddess and mermaid; he already looked stunned enough.

"You're incredible," Ted repeated. "Just look at you. You were stunning before, but this is... I have no words."

"This is me, Ted. All of me," Jolie said, swimming close. "I love you, Ted. I want to be with you. Will you give us a chance?"

Ted visibly blanched at her words and Jolie's stomach dropped.

"Jolie... no, I can't possibly. I don't deserve you. I'm a mere mortal. You're a goddess. I couldn't possibly..."

Jolie didn't bother to listen to anything more he had to

say. Her heart shredded, she turned and dove deep into the water, leaving him shouting after her on the beach, letting the ocean catch her tears. When Irma and Mirra caught up to her, they held her, all three in their mermaid forms, as Jolie wept her heart out. On the surface, waves raged, the sea angry as a storm raced in.

CHAPTER 33

When Ted arrived back at the Laughing Mermaid, bone tired, he half wondered if the guesthouse would still be there. When the storm had rolled in, he'd had to take shelter in the tent; the waves were too dangerous for him to try to cross the ledge to where the truck was parked. As the winds had intensified, he'd left the tent to find the small cave where Jolie had first shown him the mermaid etching. He'd sat there for what seemed like hours, his headlamp shining on the carving, sodden and sad as he went over the events of the night in his mind.

How could a woman – no, a magickal mermaid – like Jolie even give someone like him the time of day, let alone choose him as a partner? A lover? It was beyond anything he could even wrap his head around. He was punching so far above his weight he didn't even know what to do.

When she'd first kissed him, he'd been shocked to the core. Her kiss had been everything he'd dreamed of and more, and his mind had screamed at him to embrace what she'd given him.

Her love, she said. She'd told him she loved him. And he'd sent her away.

Even now, it stung, replaying the hurt in her eyes and the flip of that ruby red tail before she'd disappeared below the surface. He'd waited for a few minutes, convinced she would reappear. He'd even waded out into the water, looking for her, worried that she'd drown. Eventually it dawned on him that she was truly gone.

And that he'd finally found his mermaid.

As he'd studied the carving while the storm raged outside, he could have sworn it began to morph and move. The mermaid danced with the man under the stars, they embraced, they even had mermaid children swimming around them. It was as if the carving was trying to tell him what could be his if he'd only accept what was being offered to him.

For a while he was fairly certain he was delirious. When the storm finally abated, Ted pulled himself from the cave – stumbling because his feet had fallen asleep – and began the task of cleaning up the mess on the beach. Their tent had been scattered to the water's edge and the hammocks were shredded. Ted slowly packed everything up, making trip after trip across the narrow ledge, leaving no trace behind. For anyone who visited, there would be no evidence they were ever there.

Or that he'd left his heart behind on the beach.

Now, he stood at the entrance to the villa, having no energy left to unpack the truck. Silently, he padded softly to Jolie's door and knocked, waiting and willing her to open it. Finally, when no answer came, he turned – and jumped.

"You're home."

"Irma. You scared me," Ted said.

"Come with me, Ted. It's time we had a little chat."

"But… um, I need to speak with Jolie. Is she here?"

"She's gone, Ted."

"What do you mean, gone?"

"Come with me," Irma said, and left him, assuming he would follow. She was right; there was no way he could refuse her request. Ted followed her outside and down the winding path that led to the beach. There he found her sitting in a low-slung chair, a bottle of whiskey and two glasses on the table. The sun, having just decided to wake up, was showing its first tender rays across the water.

"You look like you could use a drink," Irma said, pouring a shot of whiskey in his glass. "Here you go."

Ted eyed the glass dubiously. "I fear that's what landed me in this mess."

"Still not a believer, eh? Drink up. You'll need it." At Irma's harsh tone, Ted raised an eyebrow and took a swig of his whiskey. It burned going down, but he relished the pain. It was the only thing he could feel at the moment.

"Where did Jolie go? Is she safe?"

"She's safe. It pleases me that that's the first thing you ask. It appears you're not completely the asshole I was beginning to think you are. Maybe you're just stupid, then?"

Ted was honestly shocked by the words coming out of Irma's mouth. She'd always been so kind and full of grace with him – but this was another side of her altogether. He

TRICIA O'MALLEY

supposed it made sense. A mama would always protect her own.

"I'm not an asshole," Ted said, taking a smaller sip this time, his eyes out on the ocean. "But, yes, I may have been stupid in this case."

"At least you can see your faults. Do you want to tell me what happened?"

It surprised Ted that he did, indeed, want to tell her everything. So, he did, right from the start all the way up to the hours he'd spent sitting and staring at the rock carving. By the time he'd finished, she'd refilled his glass for him and was staring at him with a mixture of pity and sadness.

"Why don't we discuss a few of the finer points of this?"

"Sure," Ted said, holding the glass to his throbbing forehead.

"Let's start with what seems to be your biggest hurdle. You don't believe we're mermaid."

"You too?" Ted exclaimed, looking up in shock. His shoulders hunched at Irma's look of disgust as she shook her head at him. "Right, duh. Of course you'd be mermaid. Jolie didn't just drop from the sky. Right?"

"No, Ted, Jolie did not just drop from the sky. I birthed her through many hours of labor. That means Mirra is also mermaid. You know our secret now. You've been deemed trustworthy. Which means you're now part of the circle. What will you do with it?"

"Do?" Ted's mouth worked, but he didn't know what to say. His normally agile mind was slowed by exhaustion and alcohol.

"Will you betray us? Out us to the world?"

"Oh my god, I would never! No, please don't think that of me. I would never bring harm to you." Ted reeled back, spilling some of his whiskey on his knee, as he looked at Irma in shock.

"Good. I'm happy to hear that. Jolie has chosen to trust you, which means we do as well. I hope you don't give us reason to feel that is a mistake."

"No, never. Irma, I will take this to the grave with me."

"Do you believe us now? There's nothing more we can say or do to make you believe. You got the full show last night. Even Mother Moon danced for you. This was it. All the bells and whistles. Jolie gave you her all. If you don't believe in us after this, nothing we can say or do will change your mind."

"I need a moment." Ted stood and walked slowly to the water's edge, looking out at the horizon.

Jolie was a mermaid. Mermaids were actually real. His deepest wish was coming – no, *had* – come true. When he realized he was unconsciously searching the horizon, hoping Jolie would pop up out of the smooth morning water, Ted understood that he'd come to accept what had once just been a fantastic dream. Turning, he made his way back up the sand to where Irma sat patiently waiting for him.

"I believe. I'm sorry I didn't at first. It's a lot to take in, I'll admit…" He stopped talking when Irma swiped a tear from her eye. "Oh… please don't cry. I'm so sorry I've caused you pain. I'm such an idiot."

"It's fine. It's fine. I've just really wanted this for Jolie, and I was nervous you'd come back up here and call us all a bunch of crazy fools and catch the next flight out of here."

"No, I'm the only fool here."

"Right you are on that one, my boy. Shall we see what we can do to fix it?"

"Please. Will you help me?"

"I guess I need to know what you're looking for first? My daughter bared her soul to you. Taking the mermaid part out of it, she still has feelings. What happened there?"

"The truth?"

"Please."

"I can't believe that a goddess like her would ever pick someone like me."

"Why?" Irma's gaze was unwavering, making Ted feel like she could read his soul.

"Well… shit. It's so dumb and I thought I'd outgrown it. I guess the wounds run deep. I don't feel like I'm a good enough man for a woman as amazing as Jolie," Ted admitted, then explained to Irma about the bullying he'd endured in his past.

"But, Ted, in some ways that's a good thing," Irma said at the end of his story. "That means you'll never really hurt her because you understand that type of pain. You'll never belittle her or make her feel like she's not as awesome as she is. You're perfect for her."

"I tried to keep my distance…" Ted whispered.

"Do you have feelings for her, Ted?"

"I do."

"Tell me why. Because she's beautiful?"

"Oh, that's just the icing on the cake. She's smart, and funny, and silly. I love when she laughs so hard that she snorts and then gets mad at herself. She's surprisingly capable, and she's a risktaker. Her recall for stories is fantastic. I just like her... all of her. Every time I see her, my world lights up and I want to tell her about my day."

"Ah." Irma pressed a hand to her chest. "That makes a mother's heart happy. Jolie's a powerful force. But most men have never bothered to see below the surface. She loves you."

"I love her back."

"Don't you think you'd better tell her that?"

"I'd like to. If I can find her."

"She can be found. I happen to be very good at locating wayward daughters. The teen years were hell," Irma laughed.

"I... well, I'd like to plan something special, actually. After everything she tried to show me, I think it's important that I show her just what she means to me. Everything is so raw and fresh right now. I'm worried she won't believe me..."

"Oh, you want to romance her? Even better. What's your idea?"

Irma leaned in and they began to plan.

CHAPTER 34

*I*t had been a week.

An entire week since she'd left Ted at the shoreline, gaping at her like a fish out of water, and she hadn't heard a word from him.

"Jolie. Don't you want to know how he's doing?"

"No, I do not." Jolie sniffed and turned a page of one of the gossip magazines Mirra had brought her.

"You can't stay here forever."

"Why not? It's lovely here."

She'd holed up in one of Prince's vacation villas, not having to say anything other than she had a broken heart. Aside from making sure Prince didn't try to kill Ted, she'd had no contact with the outside world. Every day, she swam in the pool and watched mindless television, but refused to set foot back in the sea.

"It's lovely here. But it's not home."

"It could be. Maybe I could buy it."

"And what? Putter around alone up here on the hill? What have you even been doing with your time?"

Jolie wasn't about to tell Mirra what she'd really been doing. She wasn't ready to tell anyone. But after one too many hours of television, she'd finally given up, pulled out a pad of paper, and started writing. Surprising even herself, the words had flowed out of her and she'd filled four notebooks full of stories and ideas. Maybe a few plotlines centered around shoving a hapless male over the side of a cliff, but she could edit those if needed. Maria had been kind enough to keep her supplied with meals, clucking over her like a concerned hen, until Jolie finally had to send her away so she could dive back into her writing.

"It's none of your business."

"Well, consider this an intervention. Go shower. You stink. Put on something presentable. I need you to come help me with a vacation rental for Sam."

"Why can't Sam do it?"

"Because she's celebrating an anniversary with Lucas and guests are arriving. Come on, please?"

"Fine. But I don't want to talk about Ted. Promise?"

"Hand to heart," Mirra said.

Jolie had stalked off to shower and change into a simple tank dress. Now, she stayed silent as Mirra chattered away. She stayed true to her promise not to speak of Ted, only filling Jolie in on the island gossip on the drive to the villa. Once they'd parked, Mirra opened the door and grabbed one of the bags from the back. "Hey, can you grab the other bag?" Mirra asked, then she strode to the front door and unlocked it.

Jolie met her at the door.

"Oh shoot," Mirra said. "I forgot my phone. It had the instructions on what rooms to put everything in. I'll just grab it – go drop that in the kitchen, will you?" Mirra handed her the other bag and nudged her to the kitchen, closing the front door behind her.

"Jeez, it's freezing in here," Jolie said, walking down a narrow hallway to what was presumably the kitchen area. "Their air conditioning costs are going to be insane if they leave it on like th–"

Jolie shrieked and dropped both bags at her feet. Something splintered, but she didn't care. All she could do was look around in awe at the scene before her.

The living area was a wide-open space combining both the kitchen and sitting space. All the curtains had been drawn shut over the windows, and twinkly lights had been strung up in crisscross patterns all across the room. In the corner stood an actual Christmas tree, decorated with ornaments. Ted stood in front of the tree, looking amazing, holding a basket in his arms.

And from the ceiling, what looked like little bits of confetti dropped to the floor.

The second shock hit her. "Is that snow?" Jolie gasped, looking up to where a machine spurted out little flecks of snow that danced into the air and fell lazily to the floor before melting immediately. "Did you bring me snow?"

Tears pricked her eyes as she finally looked up at Ted, who looked much too damn handsome for how mad she was at him.

"I did. Well, the best I could. Even with the air conditioning as low as it can go, it still melts."

"It's… oh, this is incredible, Ted." Jolie walked into the room, her entire body shaking with nerves, as she looked up to the snow. He'd somehow managed to backlight it and it looked magickal as it dropped through the air.

As if reading her mind, he smiled nervously at her and said, "I thought since you showed me your magick, I would do my best to show you some of mine."

"Oh," Jolie whispered, her heart pounding so hard in her chest she wondered if he could hear it.

"I have something else for you," Ted said, holding out the basket, "if you'll take it."

"I suppose it won't hurt to look," Jolie sniffed, trying to hold onto her anger when all she wanted to do was dance gleefully across the room and catch snowflakes on her tongue.

"Careful," Ted said as he handed it off, and her arms drooped with the weight of it. Something shifted inside and her eyes darted to Ted's.

"Is something moving in there?"

"I guess you'll have to see." Ted shrugged a shoulder.

Jolie looked around for a place to sit, but the furniture had been pulled from the room – probably to prevent water damage from the snow, she thought. Instead, she crouched on the floor and opened the lid of the basket. Inside a bundle of fur rolled over and looked up at her, pushing its nose up at her face before tentatively stretching up and looking over the side of the basket.

"You got me a puppy?" Jolie said, her voice going up an octave.

"You said you'd always wanted one. I asked Irma's permission. She went with me to the shelter so we could pick out the right one. She promises this one is perfect. He has the sweetest disposition."

"She doesn't care about having it at the house?"

"She thinks Pipin will like having a neighbor dog to pal around with on the beach."

The puppy almost fell out of the basket in his attempt to lick her hand and she picked him up, clutching him to her chest.

"It's a boy?"

"It is."

"Oh." Jolie's heart did a little flip in her chest as her tears spilled over. She looked around the room, and then down at the puppy in her arms. He'd remembered what she'd said she had always wanted. And he probably understood now why she couldn't travel. Instead of trying to force her into his world, he'd brought it to her.

"Jolie, will you listen to what I have to say?"

"Yes, I will," Jolie said. She plopped cross-legged on the floor to cradle the pup in her arms.

Ted came and sat down in front of her, mirroring her pose, but still giving her space. Overhead, the snow continued to fall around them, and the twinkle lights sparkled. For the first time ever, Jolie felt totally out of her element. She wondered if what she felt now was even a smidgen of what Ted had felt when she'd dragged him to Siren City. Guilt flooded her.

"I'm sorry I shocked you like that. I should have prepared you for it," Jolie said before Ted could speak.

He paused with his mouth open, and then closed it. "Thank you for that. If I can just get through this? I prepared this speech; I've been practicing it."

Of course he had, Jolie thought, bending to kiss the puppy's head.

"First of all, I'm sorry. One hundred times over, I'm sorry."

Jolie lifted her head to speak, but snapped her mouth shut at his look. Right, no interruptions.

"It was such a shock to me; I was just bowled over. All of it. Not even just the mermaid part, but the fact that you had feelings for me too. I never, ever, imagined someone as amazing as you would even consider me as her partner. It seemed too good to be true. It made me feel like I was back in school – being set up for another joke, to be laughed at."

"Oh, Ted." Jolie looked at him, stricken.

"I understand that wasn't your intent. But it was a lot to process at once. I want you to know, though, that I too have been developing feelings for you for quite some time."

"Is that so?" Jolie felt a shiver of excitement work through her.

"It is. And I tried to fight them. I kept firmly putting you into a role as my employee. And, I didn't want to piss Irma off."

"She can be quite formidable."

"So I've learned."

"Scared ya, did she?"

"Let's just say we had a come-to-Jesus talk."

"Go on…"

"I was ready to admit my feelings for you. Yes, I know it didn't seem like that, but I was going to work around to it in my own slow plodding way. But when you showed me you were mermaid? Oh, that was tough."

"Why? Why exactly?" Jolie didn't want to put words

in his mouth. She stroked the puppy's coat as it fell asleep in her arms.

"Because you leveled up on me. You went from this amazing woman to an actual goddess. How could I ever be worthy?"

"Because you *are* worthy. And because I chose you. Your heart is pure gold," Jolie whispered.

"I may never get the chance to prove I'm worthy of you, Jolie, but I'd like a lifetime of trying if you'll have me."

"Oh." Jolie blinked against the tears that began to fall for real now. "I'd like that."

"I have one more gift for you, if you'll accept it."

"More? How could there possibly be more? You gave me snow," Jolie laughed, delighted at what was happening.

"Bear with me; I've never done this before," Ted said, shifting so that he kneeled awkwardly before her. From behind his back he pulled out the oracle necklace and dangled it in front of her. "Jolie, I love you so much. I will spend my life proving it to you. I'll do everything I can to make you proud to have me on your arm. Or… by your tail. Or, you know – oh god." Ted blushed, shaking his head sadly at his awkwardness.

"Yes, Ted." Jolie leaned forward, laughing and crying at the same time while he kissed her. "Yes, I accept your proposal."

"Oh, thank god," Ted said, kissing her over the sleepy pup in her arms, and all the anger and angst she'd been carrying all week left her in one fell swoop. Desperate to touch him, she reached out to wrap her arms around him, but the puppy yelped in annoyance.

"Oh, whoops. This one doesn't like to share." Jolie pulled back, laughing down at the puppy in her lap.

"May I?" Ted asked, holding the necklace up.

"Please," Jolie said, and bowed her head while Ted placed the jewelry around her neck. The pendant settled between her breasts, warming her heart.

"Ted, you know I can't travel, right? I'm kind of stuck here. There are certain downfalls to being a mermaid."

"I've decided I've had more than enough of snowy winters. And if you take me to visit Siren City once in a while, I think I'll be set for traveling."

"Do you really mean it? It doesn't bother you?"

"If you don't mind that I pop home once in a while to visit my family, then no, it doesn't bother me."

"Will they think I'm weird to not travel there?"

"Nah. I'll go during your high season and explain how busy you are."

"Oh my goddess, I can't believe this is happening." Jolie grabbed him and kissed him once more. She deepened the kiss, wanting his hands on her – then the front door flung open.

"You'd better be decent," Mirra called.

"Damn it, Mirra." Jolie pulled back. "Ever think of knocking?"

"Oh hush; you have your whole life to jump this man. But I never get to see snow!" Irma and Mirra dashed into the room, twirling in delight while the puppy roused himself to bark at the sudden intrusion. Together, they all jumped and danced in the snow, and Ted pulled Jolie into his arms.

Mirra stopped, looking down at the little puppy racing in circles, trying to nip snowflakes from the air.

"What are you going to name him?"

"Snowball. Because Ted gave me something I couldn't give myself."

EPILOGUE

*J*olie rolled over in bed, naked in the sheets, and stretched. It had been months since the fateful night Ted had proposed to her, and they still hadn't sated each other's needs.

Ted could be slow and sometimes maddeningly methodical in day-to-day life, and – well, as it turned out, that trait carried over into the bedroom. Each day he settled in to spend some of his time driving Jolie to the brink of madness, and Jolie was equally as addicted to bringing him to the edge. Mirra had been right about intimacy and sex, Jolie mused, standing and padding naked out into the living area.

They'd rented a small villa together, just a few houses down the beach from the Laughing Mermaid, until they could decide if they wanted to buy a place or build. Snowball had grown into his paws, and now spent his mornings racing over the sand to visit Pipin and eventually curl up at Irma's feet in her kitchen. Jolie half-suspected the dog was more Irma's than hers, but she didn't mind sharing, so long as Snowball was happy.

"Good morning, sleepy…" Ted trailed off as he caught sight of her naked body. Jumping up from the stool where he drank his coffee, he rounded the kitchen island and wrapped his arms around Jolie, backing her against the wall and kissing her until she was breathless.

"And a good morning to you," Jolie breathed, feeling all the parts of him that were now wide awake.

"I don't know how I get any work done around you. All I want to do is touch you," Ted said, kissing the nape of her neck and sending tendrils of heat whispering across her skin.

"I don't see anything wrong with that." Jolie gasped as his hands crept up and cupped her breasts, his fingers absentmindedly stroking her nipples. She moaned, feeling heat pool in her core, and ran her hands down his chest.

"Typically I don't either," Ted said, falling into a kiss once more before pulling himself away. "But I have a surprise for you."

"Is that so? Show me," Jolie demanded. She'd come to learn that Ted loved planning little surprises for her; typically they were quite thoughtful.

"Here you go." Ted handed her a small stack of papers.

Jolie glanced at him in confusion before looking down to read what appeared to be a contract.

"Wait, is this a book contract? For you?"

"Nope, for us. Co-authors. See?" Ted leaned over and pointed to her name, listed along with information about an advance from the publishing company.

"And we get an advance?" Jolie's voice rose.

"Yes, we get an advance – if you like the deal. We can negotiate."

"I'm going to be an author? I'll make real money?"

"I mean, it's hard to say how much you'll make. Our subject matter is going to be very niche. But yes, you'll be a real published author."

"Oh my goddess!" Jolie shrieked and threw her hands up. "Oh, now I've got three jobs to Mirra's one. She's going to be so pissed."

"Glad you're focusing on the good stuff here." Ted shook his head and Jolie dropped the papers back on the counter, walking over to wind her arms around his neck and look up into his gorgeous green eyes.

"Oh, I'm focusing on the good stuff, I promise." And with that, Jolie tugged him back to the bedroom just to emphasize her point.

She was an author now, after all.

———

I HOPE my books have added a little magick into your life. If you have a moment to add some to my day, you can help by telling your friends and leaving a review. Word-of-mouth is the most powerful way to share my stories.

Thank you.

Tricia O'Malley

Read on for a taste of Too Good to Be True, Book five in the Siren Island series.

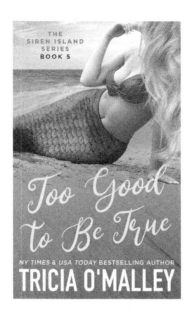

Available from Amazon

**The following is a sneak peak from
Too Good to Be True**

Book 5 in the Siren Island Series

CHAPTER 1

*M*irra drifted with the current, enjoying the pull of the water as it flowed over her fin, stretching her arms in front of her to revel in the weightlessness of being surrounded by the sea. Here – she was home. It was only on land where she was constantly awkward, running into corners, and blushing when someone paid her too much attention. Her twin sister, Jolie, had confidence in spades while Mirra preferred to take a quieter backseat to her antics. It was only when she returned to the sea did Mirra feel like she could truly be herself and there she found the confidence she wished for on the shore.

Now, diving deep, she pulled herself from her meditation and let herself tune into the flow and the rhythm of the ocean surrounding her. It wasn't difficult to do, or not for a mermaid at least, and she was able to read the energy of the reefs around her to see if there was anything in distress. Periodically, Mirra would spend an entire evening searching the reefs for turtles caught in fishing line, or cleaning up trash stuck on the corals. She considered it almost an underwater gardening of sorts, and liked to keep the reefs around her island as tidy as could be.

When the distress call came, Mirra's head went up. Closing her eyes, she sent out her power, like a sonar wave of magick, to find out where she was needed. The call went up again and tears spiked Mirra's eyes as she surged forward, faster than any fish, and barreled toward where her friends were in trouble. Heart pounding in her chest, she came to an abrupt stop as she stumbled on the source of the call.

Dolphins caught in a large-scale commercial fishing net. An entire pod of them, mothers and babies alike, all screamed to her for help. Desperate, Mirra surfaced briefly, taking a quick scan of the situation. The boat was large, a whaler type ship, and she knew they hadn't caught the dolphins by accident. Large cranes creaked as they pulled the nets in and her friends surfaced, shrieking frantically in the dark water.

Diving below the surface, Mirra circled the net, sending a blast of calming magick to the dolphins and instructing them to circle together in the middle so as not to get their fins caught in the net. Focusing, Mirra drew a silver knife from the sheath at her side, impossibly sharp and blessed with magick from Poseidon himself, and got to work. Her blade sliced neatly through the thick cable and as it snapped, the cord whipped around her middle, ensnaring her.

"Go!" Mirra urged, wrestling with the cable that bit into the flesh at her waist, "Get out of here. I'll be fine. Save yourselves!" Mirra blasted the dolphins with her urgency and they dove through the opening she'd created, streaming free from captivity and certain death. But once outside the net, they swam deep below her – far enough away from any chance of being captured again – but refusing to leave Mirra's side. Sounding the alarm, Mirra could hear them trumpeting for help from her brethren.

She gasped as the cable tightened, threatening to cut off her breath, and reeled her toward the boat. Dots sparked her vision and Mirra knew she was only moments away from death.

"Help…" Mirra whispered, struggling desperately while trying to cut the cable once more, "Please…"

Available from Amazon

AFTERWORD

Living in the Caribbean has helped to inspire my descriptions of Siren Island. If it wasn't for my love of the ocean, and the mysteries that lie within, I would never have been able to write these books. Thank you for coming along on my journey.

Have you read books from my other series? Become a Siren in our little community by signing up for my newsletter for or updates on island-living, giveaways, and how to follow me on social media!
http://eepurl.com/1LAiz.

ALSO BY TRICIA O'MALLEY

THE ISLE OF DESTINY SERIES

Stone Song

Sword Song

Spear Song

Sphere Song

———————

A completed series in Kindle Unlimited.

Available in audio, e-book & paperback!

"Love this series. I will read this multiple times. Keeps you on the edge of your seat. It has action, excitement and romance all in one series."

- Amazon Review

THE ENCHANTED HIGHLANDS

Wild Scottish Knight

Wild Scottish Love

A Kilt for Christmas

Wild Scottish Rose

"I love everything Tricia O'Malley has ever written and "Wild Scottish Knight" is no exception. The new setting for this magical journey is Scotland, the home of her new husband and soulmate. Tricia's love for her husband's country shows in every word she writes. I have always wanted to visit Scotland but have never had the time and money. Having read "Wild Scottish Knight" I feel I have begun to to experience Scotland in a way few see it. I am ready to go see Loren Brae, the castle and all its magical creatures, for myself. Tricia O'Malley makes the fantasy world of Loren Brae seem real enough to touch!"

-Amazon Review

Available in audio, e-book, hardback, paperback and is included in your Kindle Unlimited subscription.

THE WILDSONG SERIES

Song of the Fae

Melody of Flame

Chorus of Ashes

Lyric of Wind

———

"The magic of Fae is so believable. I read these books in one sitting and can't wait for the next one. These are books you will reread many times."

- Amazon Review

A completed series in Kindle Unlimited.

Available in audio, e-book & paperback!

THE SIREN ISLAND SERIES

Good Girl

Up to No Good

A Good Chance

Good Moon Rising

Too Good to Be True

A Good Soul

In Good Time

A completed series in Kindle Unlimited.

Available in audio, e-book & paperback!

"Love her books and was excited for a totally new and different one! Once again, she did NOT disappoint! Magical in multiple ways and on multiple levels. Her writing style, while similar to that of Nora Roberts, kicks it up a notch!! I want to visit that island, stay in the B&B and meet the gals who run it! The characters are THAT real!!!" - Amazon Review

---

"Not my usual genre but couldn't resist the Florida Keys setting. I was hooked from the first page. A fun read with just the right amount of crazy! Will definitely follow this series."- Amazon Review

A completed series in Kindle Unlimited.

Available in audio, e-book & paperback!

THE MYSTIC COVE SERIES

Wild Irish Heart

Wild Irish Eyes

Wild Irish Soul

Wild Irish Rebel

Wild Irish Roots: Margaret & Sean

Wild Irish Witch

Wild Irish Grace

Wild Irish Dreamer

Wild Irish Christmas (Novella)

Wild Irish Sage

Wild Irish Renegade

Wild Irish Moon

"I have read thousands of books and a fair percentage have been romances. Until I read Wild Irish Heart, I never had a book actually make me believe in love."- Amazon Review

A completed series in Kindle Unlimited.

Available in audio, e-book & paperback!

STAND ALONE NOVELS

Ms. Bitch

"Ms. Bitch is sunshine in a book! An uplifting story of fighting your way through heartbreak and making your own version of happily-ever-after."

~Ann Charles, USA Today Bestselling Author

Starting Over Scottish

Grumpy. Meet Sunshine.

She's American. He's Scottish. She's looking for a fresh start. He's returning to rediscover his roots.

One Way Ticket

A funny and captivating beach read where booking a one-way ticket to paradise means starting over, letting go, and taking a chance on love…one more time

10 out of 10 - The BookLife Prize

CONTACT ME

Love books? What about fun giveaways? Nope? Okay, can I entice you with underwater photos and cute dogs? Let's stay friends, receive my emails by signing up at my website

www.triciaomalley.com

As always, you can reach me at
info@triciaomalley.com

Or find me on Facebook and Instagram.
@triciaomalleyauthor

AUTHOR'S ACKNOWLEDGEMENT

First, and foremost, I'd like to thank my family and friends for their constant support, advice, and ideas. You've all proven to make a difference on my path. And, to my beta readers, I love you for all of your support and fascinating feedback!

And last, but never least, my two constant companions as I struggle through words on my computer each day - Briggs and Blue.